The Bistro at Holiday Bay:
Cons and Canines
by

Kathi Daley

This book is a work of fiction. Names, characters, places, and incidents either are products of the author's imagination or are used fictitiously. Any resemblance to actual events or locales or persons, living or dead, is entirely coincidental.

The Inn at Holiday Bay

Secret in the Santa

Riddle in the Review

Clue in the Carriage House

Witness in the Wedding

Christmas in the Candlelight

Secret in the Storm

Clue in the Cottage

Message in the Manuscript

Trouble in the Theatre

Evidence in the Espresso

Christmas in the Country

V in the Valentine

Kidnapped in the Kitchen

Bistro at Holiday Bay

Opera and Old Lace

Moonlight and Broomsticks

Cupid and Cool Jazz

Sunshine and Sweet Wine

Clues and Canines

Ravioli and Resolutions

Homecoming and Homicide

Mummies and Moonshine

Cons and Canines

Boy Bands and Big Plans – coming soon

Bookstore at Holiday Bay

Once upon a Mystery

Once Upon a Haunting

Once Upon a Christmas

Once Upon a Clue

Once Upon a Harvest Moon

Once Upon a Snowy Night

Once Upon a Shuttered Past – coming soon

Holiday Bay Cast

The Inn at Holiday Bay

Abby Sullivan – owner of the inn – dating Colt (Rufus – cat, Molly – dog)

Georgia Carter-Peyton – minority owner and inn manager – recently married Tanner (Ramos – dog)

Jeremy Slater – full-time inn employee

Mylie Slater – Jeremy's wife and full-time inn employee

Annabelle Cole – Jeremy's niece – lives with Mylie and Jeremy (Snow White – cat)

Danny/Daniel Alexander Slater – Mylie and Jeremy's son

Haven Hanson – full-time inn employee (Baxter – dog)

Bailey Sullivan – mysterious stranger working at the inn

Hazel Sullivan – Bailey's daughter

Police Chief Colt Wilder – Police Chief – dating Abby

(Colt's niece and nephew – Mackenzie/Mackey Hudson and Tyler Hudson)

Tanner Peyton – owner of a dog-training academy – recently married Georgia

Lonnie and Lacy Parker – Abby and Colt's best friends

(Parker Children – Michael, Matthew, Mark, Mary, Meghan, and Madison/Maddie)

Officer Alex Weston – Colt's second-in-command – dating Leo Atwell (Cooper/Coop – dog)

Officer Brax/Braxton Baker – newest officer assigned to assist Colt

Gabby Gibson – police dispatcher

The Bistro at Holiday Bay

Shelby Morris – owner of the Bistro, dating Dawson (Hennessy – cat)

Amy Hogan – Shelby's business partner and friend, head chef (Marley – cat)

Dawson Westwood – Shelby's business partner, bar manager, dating Shelby (Goliath – dog)

Nikki Peyton – waitress, backup bartender – Tanner's half-sister

Lucy Lansing – waitress – lives with Eden Halliwell

Charmaine Kettleman – waitress

Cambria – sous-chef

Rosalyn Montgomery – dining room manager

Beck Cage – PI with an office in the Bistro (Meatball – dog)

Leo Atwell – lives next to Shelby – dating Alex Weston (Fisher – dog)

Sierra Danielson – Shelby's half-sister

Sage Wilson – Shelby's half-sister

The Bookstore at Holiday Bay

Lou Prescott – owner of Firehouse Books, along with Velma (Toby – cat, Houdini – cat)

Velma Crawford – owner of Firehouse Books, along with Lou

Eden Halliwell – full-time bookstore employee

Royce Crawford – Velma's husband and member of *Murder on Tuesdays*

Cricket Abernathy – owner of All About Bluebells, along with Marnie – Thursday evening book club

Marnie Abernathy – owner of All About Bluebells, along with Cricket – Thursday evening book club

Ethel Covington – owner of A Bit of This and That – Wednesday night Senior Women's Group

Andy Anderson – owner of Surfside Deli, along with Eli

Eli Anderson – owner of Surfside Deli, along with Andy

Savannah Garrison – all three book clubs – Joel's friend

Joel Stafford – head of *Murder on Tuesdays*

George Baxter – part-time resident – *Murder on Tuesdays*

Hazel Hawthorn – longtime local – runs the local cat rescue – Thursday evening book club

Chapter 1

"Hey, Shelby, I just wanted to let you know that Alex and Leo are here with Coop and Fisher."

I raised a finger toward my friend and waitress, Nikki Peyton, who stood just beyond my office door, indicating that I needed a moment. Alex Weston was an officer for the Holiday Bay Police Department and Colt's second-in-command, Coop was her dog, Leo Atwell was Alex's boyfriend and my closest neighbor, and Fisher was his dog. "I'm on hold with the woman from the Holiday Bay High School Booster Club. Can you set up a table for six on the rooftop? I know the rooftop isn't officially open for the season until Friday, but since it's such a nice day and Leo's birthday, I think it will be perfect, especially with the presence of multiple dogs."

"Yeah, no problem. I'll set a table, explain that you might be a few minutes late, and then get Alex and Leo seated. Is Dawson joining you?" she asked about my bar manager and boyfriend, Dawson Westwood.

I nodded. "Yes, as soon as Dawson finishes showing his house, he'll head this way. Goliath and Meatball are with him, so we'll need to add two more doggy lunches to the ones I already told the kitchen about. I guess, plan for six humans and four dogs."

"And the other two humans besides you, Dawson, Alex, and Leo?"

"Sage and Garret will be joining us." Sage Wilson was my half-sister, and Garret Hemingway was her partner in the line of outdoor wear the team manufactured right here in Maine.

"I heard that Sage was designing t-shirts for the dog rescue," Nikki said, referring to the dog rescue Alex and Leo founded a little over a year ago. They were building a new facility to house the dogs while they waited for foster parents or adoption. The dogs were currently housed on Leo's property, which greatly limited the number of canines he could rescue at the current time.

"She is," I answered. "Alex and Leo wanted something to give to the volunteers, fosters, and donors who committed to a specific dollar amount. I'm not sure how it all works, but I know Sage has samples of a couple different options to show the pair."

"I guess they'll need to get the shirts ordered sooner rather than later. I heard Alex and Leo broke ground on the building last week."

"They did. The fencing is already in, and I know there are plans for both indoor and outdoor play and socialization areas. I think the facility is going to be something really special."

I held up a finger once again as someone came on the line. Nikki paused and waited for me to speak with the caller. "False alarm," I said. "Rather than being Charise, the woman who initiated the call wanted to tell me it would just be another minute."

"Why don't you just have this woman call you back when she's free," Nikki wondered. "It seems rude that she had her secretary call you only to put you on hold."

"Housekeeper. Charise doesn't work, so it was her housekeeper who called me. And yes, having her call me if Charise wasn't ready to talk was rude. I'm tempted to merely hang up, but by this point, I have a lot of time invested in this call and want to find out whatever this woman is calling me to rearrange."

Nikki shrugged. "I guess I get that to a point, but experience has shown that if you're overly accommodating, the customer tends to take advantage of that, and we'll be dealing with her changes right up to the last minute."

Thinking back to some of the other high-maintenance customers we'd dealt with, I knew Nikki had a valid point. Still, it was early, and there was time to make changes, so I figured we would. "Be sure to bring water bowls out for all the dogs in addition to whatever doggy treats Amy and Cambria cook up," I said, veering the subject away from my tendency to want to overplease.

"I will. I think it's fun that Amy and Cambria are creating a special meal for the dogs." Amy Hogan was the Bistro's chef, and Cambria was Amy's sous chef. "Nick and I have talked about adopting a midsized dog now that he finished the house he's been renovating."

"I heard that you and Nick have decided to move into it rather than flip it."

"We did. It's perfect for us. Good size. Nice area. And since Nick did most of the labor, we got into it for a steal." Nick Jergenson was Nikki's live-in boyfriend. "Maybe I'll talk to Leo about keeping his eyes open for a dog who would be a good match for us. Since Nick has his own business and spends most of his day at whichever project he's working on, I know he'd like a dog who would fit in well on the construction site."

"Like Lonnie's Sadie," I said. Lonnie Parker was my contractor, and Sadie was his dog. Not only did she go everywhere with him, but she also knew and followed all the rules. She knew which areas were safe to hang out in and which to avoid.

"Or Beck's Meatball, who just sits in his bed next to Beck's booth," Nikki added.

Beck Cage was a local PI who'd claimed a booth in the bar as his office. He brought his English Bulldog, Meatball, to work with him most days.

Dawson's Great Dane mix, Goliath, and Meatball had been rescued from the shelter on the same day and were the best of buddies even though one dog was huge and the other had legs so short that it was necessary to walk really slow for him to keep up.

"Has Nick found another house to flip?"

Since arriving in Holiday Bay, Nick had purchased and renovated two homes in the area and subsequently decided to stay. He was very good at what he did and consistently took the time necessary to ensure that everything came out just right.

"He has," Nikki answered. "It's a rundown cottage on the beach about forty miles up the coast from Holiday Bay. The location is perfect for someone looking for isolation but not the best place for someone who has kids or is outgoing and wants to be part of a community. I was concerned that the pool of buyers would be limited due to the isolation, but Nick seemed to think there would be introverted types who would consider a small two-bedroom bungalow on the sand the perfect home. Or maybe vacation home," she added.

Being so isolated wouldn't be my thing, but I could see how the quiet would appeal to some.

"Ms. Morris?" the woman I'd been holding for inquired.

"Yes, this is Shelby," I replied as Nikki scurried off to ensure that Alex and Leo were settled.

"Thank you for holding. I'm afraid it's been one of those days where everything that can go wrong has gone wrong," Charise Bowden informed me.

"I understand and was happy to hold. So how can I help you?"

The woman launched into a long dialogue about minor changes she wanted to make to the plans for the luncheon she'd scheduled for mid-May. It was still a month until the luncheon was to take place, so the changes wouldn't be a problem, but I kept Nikki's suggestion in mind about not giving the woman the idea that she could change things up whenever she had an urge. Since I wanted to be sure she got it right this time, I took my time and asked lots of questions to ensure that she'd really thought things through. She assured me she'd figured out exactly what she wanted, so I carefully wrote detailed notes. The luncheon was to honor the high school booster club's members, and I knew that it was events such as this where a lot of fundraising and volunteer recruitment took place.

"I can assure you that we will take your requests into account when planning the menu," I said once I'd read the list of changes back to her. "But please keep in mind that there are specialty items on the list that will need to be ordered well ahead of time, so this truly does need to be the last alteration."

"It will be, although we need to discuss the dessert."

By the time the woman had finally disconnected the call, Dawson had texted to let me know he'd returned from showing prospective tenants the house he planned to rent out now that he'd officially moved in with me. Since Nikki had informed me that Sage and Garret had also arrived, I expected that the trio would keep Alex and Leo company.

"Hey, everyone," I greeted Alex, Leo, Sage, and Garret. "Where's Dawson? I thought that he was here."

"He is, but shortly after Nikki dropped off our beverages and an appetizer platter, Beck texted Dawson and asked if he could come downstairs and look at something," Alex explained. "Dawson said he'd be right back, so I figured we could look at the samples Sage brought while we wait."

"That sounds like a good plan." I picked up a crab wonton and dipped it in Amy's special sauce.

"You should try the calamari," Sage suggested. "The calamari itself is good as usual. Fresh and lightly breaded. But what makes this calamari so special is the dipping sauce. It's delicious. Unlike anything I've ever tried."

I picked up a large piece of calamari and dipped it in the sauce. "This is good. It's sweet and spicy and somewhat tangy all at the same time. I wonder what is making it tangy. Plum?"

"I'm not sure, but it's delicious," Sage said. "Maybe Amy will share her secret with us if we ask nicely."

I wasn't so sure about that. Amy tended to protect her secrets, especially when it came to something original she'd developed herself.

I took another bite, and then everyone turned their attention to Sage, who reached into the bag she'd placed on the floor near her feet. "Basically, there are two options, and in my opinion, each option has a benefit not provided by the other. The first option is a high-quality t-shirt with a crew neck and is designed with a loose fit, which I feel will accommodate most body shapes. The t-shirts feature a pocket on the left side with your logo prominently displayed just above it." She held up a sample t-shirt in blue and another one in black. "You can choose almost any color, and I brought a color guide for you to look at, but I brought these popular options. The t-shirts come in extra small to triple extra-large."

She handed one of the t-shirts to Alex and the other to Leo.

"They are made of a good quality material," Alex said as she rubbed the fabric between her fingers. "And they should maintain their shape even after laundering. While I believe these would be perfect for the volunteers and foster parents, I have reservations about the donors. Given that some of them have made large contributions, I imagine they might be more apt to wear something more stylish."

"I agree," Sage said as she bent over to take something out of the bag. "The second option is this polo-style shirt. It likewise has a pocket on the left side, along with the logo for the rescue. The polo shirts have a collar and three buttons at the neck, and they are a bit more form-fitting than the t-shirts." She held up a black polo as well as a blue one. "Since the polos are somewhat more stylish than the t-shirts and are therefore more likely to be worn in a public setting, I can see how they might serve as a marketing source. And the polos are versatile. I can see people wearing this shirt with jeans or slacks or even a skirt, shorts, or khakis. Of course, the downfall of the polo is that the fit may not flatter certain body types, which is, of course, the upside of the t-shirt."

"What about gifting the volunteers and foster parents the t-shirt and then offering our donors the option of choosing either the polo shirt or the t-shirt," Leo suggested.

"We could do that, although it would create a small increase in the price per unit. Still, if you're expecting to give these shirts to upper-end donors, then offering them an option might be your best option, and I'm sure we can work out a deal." Sage looked at Garret, who didn't respond verbally but nodded.

"When will you need to know?" Alex asked.

Sage answered. "It depends on what you end up ordering, but I think we can fulfill most orders within a month of receiving the specifics."

Alex, Leo, Sage, and Garret continued to discuss costs, availability, and options for future orders while we waited for Dawson. Nikki came by and refilled our beverages, and while she was at the table, she let me know that Dawson was on his way up and that the meal Amy had planned would be delivered shortly after that.

Once Dawson arrived, Sage pulled another t-shirt out of her bag and handed it to him. I figured she was showing him the t-shirts she'd previously shown to Alex and Leo, but then Dawson grinned.

"That's Goliath," he said.

"It is," Sage agreed as Dawson ran a thumb over the machine-stitched logo of his dog featured on the casual beach line that Sage and Garret had been working on. "Garret and I have been going round and round about what to call our line of beachwear. The line will be casual, featuring t-shirts, tank tops, shorts, and swimwear. We wanted a name and logo to represent the line that was casual and friendly as well. We struggled to come up with the perfect name and image and tried out a bunch of ideas. Then Shelby and I took Goliath for a walk on the beach several weeks ago when you were busy in the bar, and the big guy was so happy to be out on the sand that he rolled over and over again and again in the sand. When Goliath sat up, he was covered from head to paw in white sand but was so happy. He had this sloppy grin on his face that was just adorable. I snapped a photo and sent it to Garret, and he thought it was perfect. Sandy Dog Casual Beachwear was born, and our beach line had a name and a mascot.

Dawson grinned. "That's awesome. I love it." He looked at Goliath, who, along with the other three dogs, were watching the exchange. "What do you think, big guy? You're famous."

Goliath barked once, and we all laughed. Sage indicated that they'd have samples of all the clothing in the line featuring the logo within the next few weeks, and she'd be sure that Dawson and I received a sample of everything they planned to offer. The conversation had branched off from there until Alex eventually asked Dawson how his house showing had gone.

"It went well. The couple I showed the property to expressed a willingness to start with a year-long lease but shared that the ultimate goal was to have a longer lease that might lead to a purchase. The husband is in a garage band and was excited about the soundproof room, and the wife is into crafting and thrifting and loved that there was both a garage and a workshop."

"Does the couple have kids?" I asked.

"No," Dawson answered. "They do have three dogs and admitted that they'd had a hard time finding a landlord willing to rent to a couple with three dogs, but I assured them that I was fine with the pups as long as they cleaned up after their canine family members and repaired any damage that may occur. I actually think the pro-dog policy may have sealed the deal. The couple took an application with them rather than filling it out at the house, but they said that they'd drop it by the bar by the end of the day."

"That's great," Sage said. "Shelby and I are happy to welcome you as a permanent roommate."

While Sage didn't actually live in Holiday Bay full-time, after agreeing to open a manufacturing facility for her line of outdoor wear in Maine and subsequently breaking up with her boyfriend, Scot, who she'd lived with in Los Angeles, she'd spent a lot more time at the house the two of us had inherited along with our third half-sister, Sierra Danielson. I wasn't sure Sage would ever make the move permanent, but I was happy that she seemed to be around much more than she had in the past.

Nikki and Amy came out with the main course, which looked as delicious as the appetizers were. The conversation seemed to naturally migrate toward food, dining, and the cooking show our mutual friend, Georgia Carter-Peyton, would be filming during the second week of May. Georgia was the hostess of *Cooking with Georgia*, a show produced by a local cable television station. The show had a local following, but her producer had big plans for her franchise and had asked her to write a cookbook. The special she'd be filming had been specifically developed to promote the cookbook's launch around Memorial Day.

Once the subject of food had been exhausted, I asked Alex and Leo about the rescue itself and their progress with the facility's construction, which I knew they'd just broken ground on.

"It's going well so far," Leo informed us. "I realize it's early in the construction process, but I feel confident we're off to a good start. After encountering a few minor glitches, the permit process went surprisingly fast, and Cayson seems to have managed to hire a full crew."

Cayson Boston was a local who grew up in the Holiday Bay area before moving to Baltimore, where he fell in with a bad crowd. He was convicted of killing a man during a robbery and was sent to prison. He somehow managed to get out of prison this past fall after receiving an early release. I still wasn't sure of the series of events that not only led to his release but also to the expulsion of his record. I didn't have enough of the story to decide whether he'd killed the man during the robbery or had been set up as he insisted he had, but I did know that he'd been a good neighbor, so despite my curiosity about the whole thing, I'd learned to get on just fine with the guy.

"I heard that you've had some pushback from certain segments of our town over your decision to hire Boston as your contractor for the rescue," Garret said.

"It is a fact that not everyone is happy about our choice," Leo responded. "Gavin Houghton has been vocal about the fact that he isn't happy that there are Holiday Bay residents who have welcomed a convicted killer into our town, and Lucas Manfield went so far as to hang signs near our construction site with the words 'killer go home' in bright red." Gavin Houghton was the town manager, and Lucas Manfield was a contractor I knew had put in a bid to build the facility Cayson had ultimately been hired to construct. "Having said that, I've found the majority of the individuals we're working with appear to be willing to keep an open mind as we move forward. In my experience, Cayson seems to be a good guy, and so far, he's proven to be a hard worker. He seems to know his stuff, and I feel that he has the skill set needed to do what we need to have done. Plus, I, for one, am a firm believer in second chances."

"I heard that the guy has maintained his innocence from the beginning," Dawson said.

"He has," Alex confirmed. "While I dug into things a little before Leo and I decided to hire him for the rescue project, I didn't delve too deeply. I must say, however, that his ability to work out a deal that basically wiped the whole thing from his record is odd. He either turned state's evidence and provided dirt on someone pretty big, or he really is innocent, and the DA just wanted the whole thing to go away. I'm not sure we'll ever know which is true, but to this point, the guy has been an excellent neighbor and employee."

"Are you still looking at a fall opening?" I asked.

"We are," Leo confirmed. "As long as the work on the building stays on schedule, and as long as we can find enough volunteers and employees to provide around-the-clock supervision."

"Are you planning on hiring a full staff?" Sage asked Leo.

"We plan to staff the place with a combination of both paid staff and volunteers. Since we will be housing the dogs, who will be waiting for fosters at the facility, Alex and I think it's important for a paid employee to be onsite twenty-four/seven. Beyond that, we hope to sign up enough volunteers so additional paid staff won't be necessary. At this point, I suppose all we can do is wait and see how it all works out."

"It's an ambitious project, and I admire the time and effort you've put into it," Sage said.

Charmaine Kettleman, one of my full-time year-round waitresses, came up to the rooftop to bring me a message. The message was from Charise, who requested that I call her as soon as possible. I was already beginning to regret my decision to work with the woman, but I had, so I decided to do the best job I could.

"I really should go down and return this call."

"Charise again?" Dawson asked.

I nodded. "I'm tempted to ignore Charise's message since I've already spoken to her once today, but she's the sort who will continue to call until she gets what she wants."

"And who is this Charise?" Sage asked.

"She's representing the local booster club. They're having a thank you luncheon here at the Bistro in May, and I'm afraid the woman is pretty intense about the details. I'm trying to be accommodating, but I must admit that the woman is about to test my last nerve. Nikki thinks I need to incorporate some firm boundaries into our contract, and I'm beginning to think she's right."

"I heard that the boosters are hoping to raise enough money to buy new computers for the computer lab," Leo said. "Since they're looking to purchase high-end equipment, lots of funds will need to be raised. In fact, several donors who sent checks for the rescue expressed their desire to send more if not for the huge fundraiser the high school is having."

"Why would the boosters be raising funds for computers?" I asked. "Aren't the boosters all about sports?"

"Normally, yes," Leo answered. "But I guess the teacher currently acting as head of the technology department at the high school managed to get his hands on some discretionary money last year. He planned to use the money to buy computers, but before he placed the order, the head of the athletic department came to him about using the money to send his football team to some big tournament they'd been invited to. Eventually, the teacher from the technology department agreed to a short-term loan. The money to reimburse the technology department for the loan it had extended to the football team was supposed to come from the baseball budget. But then the baseball team had a record-breaking year and needed the funds to participate in the state championship, and the loan owed to the technology department was never repaid."

"I guess that might not have gone over well with the technology folks," Garret commented.

"It didn't. Initially, there was a lot of arguing between the two department heads over the budget for the new year. But eventually, the athletic director made a deal with the technology guy, which allowed him to keep the funding he'd lined up for his teams this year."

"The athletic director agreed to ask his boosters to raise the money for the computers," I guessed.

"That's what I heard," Leo answered.

I laughed. "Who knew that high school funding could be so political."

"Oh, the funding is a big deal," Leo said. "The reality is that the need for funds greatly exceeds the funds, so finding discretionary money is like finding a treasure."

"What you're doing to help Charise with the luncheon is nice," Sage said. "And the event will be over in a few weeks, yet you'll be left with the satisfaction of knowing that you really helped those kids."

I excused myself to make the call Charmaine had come upstairs to tell me about. By the time I returned to the table, Sage and Garret had left, and Alex and Leo announced they needed to get going, too. Dawson and I wished Leo a happy birthday, and then we called Goliath and Meatball to our side and made our way downstairs. Dawson headed toward the bar with the dogs, and I headed toward the kitchen to thank Amy and Cambria for the excellent meal they'd managed to put together.

"The meal was excellent," I told my chef and her sous chef. "I really appreciate that you went to so much trouble to make something special for Leo for his birthday."

"Leo is a good guy," Amy said. "We were happy to do it. Did Dawson say how his showing went?"

"He said it went well. The couple took an application rather than filling it out on the spot, so they may have needed to check things over a bit, but Dawson said they seemed really interested in it." I paused. "Are you okay with Dawson living with us permanently?"

"Of course, I'm okay with it," Amy answered. "Dawson is an awesome guy, and it is, after all, your house. I'm eternally grateful that you have allowed me to live there rent-free for as long as you have, but I think it's time I make a move."

My smile fell. "You're moving?"

Amy smiled and glanced at Cambria. "Cam and I heard about a two-bedroom condo that unexpectedly became available in that complex west of the old seaport. The place is perfect for two people living together as roommates and even has water views."

"And the access to the beach is right across the street," Cam added.

Amy continued. "In addition to the ocean view, which is a major selling point in my opinion, it has a large living space with room for sofas and a large dining table." She paused and continued. "Like I said, the place has two bedrooms, each with its own bathroom, so we'd each have our own space."

"And the kitchen is really upper end with new appliances and a lot of counter space," Cambria contributed.

"It's a bit on the pricy side, but since I've saved up some money, I think it can work," Amy tacked on with a slight tone of hesitation.

"It sounds fabulous, but I'll miss you."

Amy came around the counter and hugged me. "And I'll miss you as well. But I'll still see you at work, and since Dawson's living with you full-time and Sage is living with you part-time, I don't think you'll get lonely. Besides, Sierra has been coming around a lot more often lately. I've thought about this a lot, and this feels like the optimum time for me to move. When this condo came available, Cam and I figured we couldn't pass up the chance to get one of those units since you have to compete with dozens and dozens of applicants most of the time."

"They are really nice, and I have heard that they rarely become available, and when they do, there's usually a lot of interest," I agreed. "When will you be moving?"

"The unit is already vacant, but the complex manager wanted to clean the carpet and paint before putting it on the rental market. Cam and I heard about it from a friend, and we went to look at it yesterday. After asking a few questions, we put a deposit down right away. The complex manager said he needed to run our credit, and if it's all okay, which we have no reason to believe it won't be, we should be able to get the keys as early as this weekend."

"Wow. That's soon. I'm really happy for you."

"I have to give notice on my place," Cambria informed me. "So we'll have to pay rent on both places for the remainder of April. I guess that will give us time to move in. I have a fair amount of junk that I should probably dispose of, but I need to go through it all."

"I understand that. Moving is a good time to purge and dispose of the old to make way for the new."

Chapter 2

After I finished chatting with Amy and Cambria I had planned to head to my office to work on payroll, but before doing so, I decided to check in with my staff downstairs. After I entered the dining room, I found a woman standing at the hostess station. "Have you been helped?"

"No, although I'm not here to eat. I'm actually looking for a man named Beck Cage. I understand that he's a private investigator."

"Beck is a private investigator and has an office of sorts here. Do you have an appointment?"

"No. I'm in town looking for my brother and have had no luck. Several people recommended Beck Cage to me, so I decided to come by and speak with him. I realize it would have been proper to call and make an appointment, but since I'm only in town today, I'm hoping that if he's in, he'll see me without an appointment."

Quite frankly, the woman looked nervous and stressed to the limit. She had dark hair and eyes, and I imagined that she would be considered attractive by most, but the burden she seemed to be carrying made her look much older than I imagined she actually was.

I smiled and tried to offer a look of support. "If Beck's here and not with a client, I'm sure he'll be pleased to speak with you. Since I just came down from upstairs, I don't know if he's in now. Why don't you take a seat while I check."

I motioned toward a row of chairs along one wall we used for customers while they waited for a table to become available and then headed toward the bar. Luckily, I found Beck sitting alone in his booth.

"I just spoke to a woman I saw standing at the hostess station in the dining room who's in town trying to find her brother. She indicated that several people suggested that she speak with you, but she's only in town today. Do you have time to talk to her?"

Beck looked down at the files in front of him. "I have a couple of active cases, but they're all pretty straightforward, so I should have time. Go ahead and show her in."

When I returned to the dining room, the woman and my waitress, Lucy Lansing, spoke as she showed Lucy a photo of a dark-haired man. I could overhear part of the conversation as Lucy explained that she hadn't lived in Holiday Bay all that long and didn't know many people but would ask some of the others. When I walked back into the room, she waved me over.

"This woman is looking for her missing brother," Lucy said.

"Yes. We've met." I looked at the woman and then held out a hand. "My name is Shelby, by the way. Shelby Morris."

"Nell Farmer."

"I'm happy to meet you, Nell. Beck is in the bar and happy to speak with you. If you'll follow me, I'll take you back."

A look of relief washed over her face. "Thank you so much. I came to Holiday Bay determined to get answers about my brother's disappearance, but it seems that I have come up cold. If I had more time, I might be able to get my answers without help, but I own a farm that demands most of my time and attention, so I really only have today."

"I understand," I said as we walked through the dining room into the bar and toward the back of the room where Beck's booth was. "Nell Farmer, this is Beck Cage."

"Your office is a booth in a bar?" she asked.

"It is," he answered with a smile. "Is that a problem?"

I could see the woman was having second thoughts, so I jumped in. "Beck may have an unconventional office space, but he's an excellent investigator," I assured the woman. When she hesitated, I motioned for her to sit and slid into the booth beside her. "Why don't you show us your photo," I suggested.

She slid the photo she'd been clutching across the table. "This is my brother, Caleb Farmer."

I recognized the man in the photo. Until three months ago, when he'd died in a fiery accident, he'd worked as a technology guy for the town. I glanced at Beck, who looked as confused as I was.

"Did you say that you were looking for your brother?" Beck asked.

She nodded. "I know Caleb is dead, or at least I know he's supposed to be dead, but I have reason to believe that he's alive. I came to Holiday Bay to look into things, but I'm just hitting one dead end after another dead end. I really want and need answers, but the amount of time I can spend here in Holiday Bay is limited since I run the farm Caleb and I inherited from our parents when they passed away. Running it is a big job, and it's only me. I truly want to find my brother, but I could only arrange for someone to take care of things for two days. I have a flight back to Nebraska this evening that I must be on, but I also hate to leave without finding the answers I came here to find. I'm hoping you can help me."

Beck took a moment, which I assumed was to gather his thoughts, and then he responded. "Caleb Farmer was killed in a vehicle accident three months ago. What makes you think he's alive?"

The woman slid a second photo across the table. "See this man in the crowd?" She pointed to a dark-haired man who could be seen in the background of a photo that featured a couple. "That's Caleb. I'm almost certain of it, yet the photo was taken just two weeks ago."

I recognized the photo of a popular "it" couple that someone had posted to social media a couple of weeks ago. The photo wasn't anything spectacular, but the couple was dressed casually in what looked to me to be an attempt to blend in with the crowd while attending a music festival.

"I remember this," I said. "It was taken at Spring Fling in Sunday River. The couple in the foreground is known for always being dressed to the nines in public situations, but in this particular photo, they look like they are trying to blend in with the crowd while wearing jeans and t-shirts. The photo was all over social media."

"Which is how I happened to see it," Nell said. "As soon as I saw the photo, I knew the man in it was Caleb and decided to look into things, but finding someone to look after my animals for even a couple of days took me more than a week. Once I finally found a good-hearted neighbor to help, I headed east, but I didn't realize when I made the plane reservation that the photo wasn't taken in Holiday Bay. I knew that Caleb lived here before his death and assumed the photo had been taken here. I may have wasted my time these past two days looking for him here."

Beck picked up the photo of the man in the crowd to get a closer look. "This man does have features similar to Caleb, but since the photo quality isn't all that good, it's hard to make out the facial features. Given the fact that your brother is known to be dead and has been declared dead for several months now, why would you think this is him?"

"It is him. I can't say how I know, but I know."

I looked at Beck. "Is this even possible? I didn't actually know Caleb. In fact, I'm quite certain I never even spoke to him, but I did read about his death in the newspaper. I seem to remember the vehicle he was driving ended up in the bottom of a ravine."

Nell jumped in. "The body was never definitively identified."

"Why not?" I asked.

Nell answered. "I was told the vehicle went off the road and over the edge in a spot with a sharp drop-off. Caleb's car apparently met with a few obstacles as it plunged into the abyss, but eventually, it landed on the rocks below. I was told the vehicle likely exploded on impact. The human remains found within the vehicle were badly damaged. So damaged, in fact, that they were unable to conclusively identify the body, but after a short investigation, it was determined that it had been Caleb driving the car, and the remains that were salvaged were sent to me. What's left of Caleb is buried on the farm where we both grew up."

Given the photo she found, even if the vehicle exploded on impact and the human remains were damaged beyond recognition, I can see how Nell might have opened the door to the possibility that her brother was actually alive. But if Caleb hadn't died in the fire and the human remains that were found belonged to someone else, why wouldn't Caleb come forward and tell someone that he was alive rather than dead?

I voiced my question aloud, and Nell answered.

"I loved my brother. After our parents died, he was all I had, and I treasured the time we spent together. But my brother was very different than me. While I'm focused and hardworking, with a love for my family and my family history, Caleb was unsettled and impulsive. He had big dreams and a tendency to act first and plan later." She paused, took a deep breath, and then continued. "Don't get me wrong, Caleb was a great guy. I don't mean to indicate otherwise, but he never fit into the roles we were destined to play the way I was."

"Roles?" I asked.

"Caleb and I grew up on the family farm, which has been in our family for six generations. It was assumed that we would take over and keep the farm going once we reached adulthood, but Caleb had other plans. My father tried to turn him into a farmer. He tried to instill a love for the land in him and to get him to understand the responsibility of a family legacy that reached back more than a century, but Caleb wanted nothing to do with the farm. Caleb didn't waste a minute, and once he turned eighteen, he enlisted in the Air Force, where he learned about computers and computer-related stuff that I could never understand. When he was discharged from the Air Force, he tried a series of computer-related jobs in several different states, but Caleb never was the sort to stay anywhere for long. Then, four years ago, our parents died in an auto accident, and the responsibility for running the family farm fell to Caleb and me. I couldn't run it without help, so I begged Caleb to come home, and he did for a while. He lasted almost a year before wanderlust grabbed him. He took off and traveled a bit. Eventually, he accepted the job here in Holiday Bay. I hate to admit it, but I haven't spoken to him since he left home. I have, however, heard through others who knew him that he appeared happy here."

"He never even went home to visit you?" I asked.

She bowed her head. "He didn't, but it wasn't his fault. I was so angry when he abruptly left me with the family farm to run alone that I told him he was no longer welcome there. I said what I did in anger and regretted it almost from the moment I said it. I wanted to mend fences, but I thought I had time to do so and hadn't taken the steps to initiate contact. When I was notified that my brother was dead three months ago, it suddenly hit me that my chance to mend fences had come to an end. I've been struggling to make sense of it all, and then two weeks ago, I saw the photo of the man at the music festival, and I just knew that Caleb wasn't gone after all." She looked at Beck. "So what do you think? Can you find my brother?"

Beck hesitated and then responded. "I can try to track down the man in the photo. I can't, however, guarantee that the man you think is Caleb is your brother."

"I understand. If nothing else, I guess I need to know one way or the other. I'm not sure what your fee is, but I'm afraid cash is tight."

"That's not a problem," Beck said. "I'm happy to take this case on pro bono. Give me a week to look into things. I'll call you every day with an update. I can't guarantee you'll get the answers you're hoping for, but as you said, any answers will be better than always wondering."

Nell thanked Beck once again and then looked at the clock on the wall. "If I don't want to miss my flight, I should head to the airport. I wish I could stay and help with the investigation, but I have animals who need to be fed."

"Understood," Beck said. He slid a new client form in front of her. "If you could just provide your contact information before you go, I'll get started."

Nell did as requested and then left.

"Do you think there's any possibility that this woman's brother is still alive?" I asked Beck after she left.

He frowned. "If I had to guess, I'd say it was unlikely, but I've seen some strange things in my life."

"I don't remember much about the accident except that it started a fire, which is how the car that ended up in a remote location was discovered. Is that right?"

Beck nodded. "There weren't any witnesses to the actual accident, so the exact series of events leading up to the crash are mostly speculation, but based on what I've read, the car seemed to have drifted off the road, eventually ending up in the bottom of the gully at the base of Juniper Ridge. The car apparently exploded on impact, which caused a brush fire that was observed by a motorist on the highway. The motorist called it in, and the local fire department responded. By the time they put the fire out and found the vehicle and the body within the vehicle, the body of the driver was so badly charred that he was unrecognizable."

"So how did they know it was Caleb?" I asked. "They must have had reason to believe that the body in the wreck was Caleb if they declared him dead."

"The vehicle's license plate was found on the ground near a tree where it's believed the vehicle temporarily became hung up before it rolled into the gorge. The investigator used the license plate number to identify the vehicle. From there, the vehicle's owner was identified. When Caleb never showed up for work, an assumption was made that he had indeed been the driver of the vehicle when it crashed."

I supposed that if Caleb's car was identified and he never showed up in his life again, an assumption could be made that the remains found had belonged to him. But I imagined that since the remains were burned beyond identification, that also opened the door to the idea that someone other than Caleb was in the vehicle when it crashed. Caleb could have lent his car to a friend, or it might have been stolen. There might have been two individuals in the vehicle that night, the driver and a passenger, who realized they were going over the side and bailed out of the car at the last minute. But if Caleb didn't die in the accident, why wouldn't he clear things up and notify the world that he was still alive?

"My gut is telling me that this investigation isn't going to turn up the results Nell is hoping for."

"I agree," Beck said. "Still, I did tell Nell I'd look into things, and that's what I plan to do."

"So what are you going to do now?"

"Head to Sunday River. I'll drive up tomorrow, take photos, and ask around."

I supposed that was as good a place to start as any. If the man in the photo was Caleb, and he was alive, then it seemed possible that he may have relocated to Sunday River after the accident. We should be able to find someone who recognized him if he had been living there for the past three months. If we successfully tracked him down, we could ask him why he'd done what he had. Not that he was likely to tell us what was going on if he was running from someone and had faked his death, but Beck could be pretty persuasive.

"Do you want some company tomorrow?" I asked. While I didn't have his experience when it came to investigating mysteries, I was comfortable talking to people, and my experience had shown that most folks were more comfortable sharing what they knew with me than they might have been if it was only a crusty retired cop doing the asking.

Beck assured me he'd love to have some company if I wanted to come, but he warned me that he planned to leave early and it would likely be a long day. I assured him I was okay with that, and we planned to meet at the Bistro at six.

Beck and I chatted a while longer, but since I really did need to process the payroll, I eventually decided to head upstairs to my office. It was hard to concentrate on something so mundane when I had a million other things on my mind, but I didn't suppose my staff would take kindly to not being paid simply because I hadn't been in the mood to run the numbers and cut their checks.

Chapter 3

It was about a four-hour drive to Sunday River, so Beck and I had plenty of time to discuss the case before we arrived. I had to admit that I'd allowed my imagination to run wild since I'd spoken to Beck the previous day and had considered many scenarios, some of which were realistic but others that weren't. I'd tried discussing my ideas with Dawson last night, but it had been busy in the bar, and by the time we got home, he was exhausted. He suggested that we talk today, but I reminded him I was meeting Beck at six. He then sat down and tried to listen to my ramblings, but I could tell he struggled to stay awake. I finally suggested that we merely go to bed.

"So, what do you think at this point?" I asked Beck as we headed west. "Do you think Caleb is alive and hiding out for some reason, or do you think the guy died in the fire as everyone assumed he did, and the guy in the photo just happens to look like him?"

Beck took a moment to respond. I was pretty sure he'd been going over the scenarios in his mind as I had, but Beck was a deliberate sort of man who would take his time considering options rather than letting his imagination go wild as mine had been. "I'm not sure. I had Dawson dig into Caleb's phone and financial records during the few lulls he had in bar traffic last evening. Since the cell phone associated with Caleb's account went offline at the time of the crash, and no one has ever added another cell phone to that account or opened a new account with his name, I'm going to assume at this point that if Caleb is still alive, he's either using a burner or he opened a different account under an alias. The man didn't have a lot of cash, but the cash he did have in his savings and checking accounts were untouched until Nell closed out the accounts after she was provided with access as his next of kin. As far as anyone knows, Caleb never returned to his apartment after the crash, and he didn't seem to have taken anything with him when he left the apartment for the last time. His toothbrush was still in the holder, and food was still in his refrigerator and cupboards."

"If he was running from someone and faking his own death was premeditated, he might have known to leave everything as it normally would have been had the accident not occurred. He may have known he needed to cut all ties to his old life."

"I suppose that could be the case," Beck admitted. "It would be the smart thing to do."

"What about calls he made or received on the day of his death?" I asked. "Do they tell you anything?"

"No," Beck answered. "The calls were routine. To and from an intern he had working with him, from a friend who later told the investigator he called Caleb to arrange a time to meet up with him for after-dinner drinks, and a call to his dry cleaner, who shared with the investigator that Caleb wanted to know if his dress shirts were ready."

"A guy who calls his dry cleaner to check on shirts on the day he dies in a fiery crash does not sound like a guy who knew he was going to die because he planned to fake his death in that crash," I pointed out. "Of course, I suppose the small details like someone making a phone call to a dry cleaner can really help sell the illusion."

"The small details can be the selling point. And it's also possible that the crash wasn't premeditated, but once it occurred, Caleb decided to take advantage of the fact that everyone would think he was dead and merely disappeared."

"Why would he do that?"

"No idea. If we can find a viable motive for the man to want to disappear, we could build a case from there."

I paused to think this over. We were sitting here discussing the possibility that Caleb could have survived the crash and was currently living out his life in another town. Maybe a better question than why was how. I tossed that question out for review.

"I've given this some thought," Beck responded. "I came up with a couple different scenarios."

"Such as?" I asked.

"Such as the scenario where Caleb was driving along the road through Juniper Ridge, drifted off onto the shoulder for some reason, realized the car was going over the edge at some point, and jumped out at the last minute."

"What about the human remains that were found? Someone died in the crash," I pointed out.

"I did consider that. I considered a few options, all of which seemed unlikely. I suppose the most logical scenario that would both allow Caleb to be alive and human remains to be found was that he was never in the car. Yesterday, we discussed the possibility that Caleb could have lent his car to someone or that someone could have stolen it. Both seem possible to me. But if we assume that Caleb actually was in the car at the time of the crash, then we need to consider the idea of a second passenger."

"Second passenger? Who?"

"I don't know, but a scenario where there were two people in the car at the time of the crash, Caleb and another as of yet unidentified male, seems to work."

"So the unidentified male was driving, and Caleb was in the passenger seat. The driver drifts off the road, and Caleb manages to escape the car through the passenger door at the last minute. Once Caleb realizes everyone thinks he's dead, he merely takes off and starts another life. Why?" I asked.

"As we discussed earlier, finding the answer to that question would go a long way toward proving or disproving the theory."

I supposed Beck had a point. "So if Caleb was in some sort of trouble and used the accident as a means of escaping his problems, could the accident have been staged?"

"It might very well have been and is a scenario that I've given a significant amount of thought to. Of course, if the whole thing was staged, then the fact that human remains were found in the vehicle takes on a whole new importance."

I turned and looked at Beck. "Do you think Caleb killed someone simply to fake his own death?"

"Not necessarily, but it is a possible scenario that needs to be considered. Of course, it's also possible that Caleb used remains from a human who was already dead."

"You're thinking grave robbery?"

Beck shrugged.

Perhaps contemplating every possible scenario hadn't been the best idea since I was suddenly creeped out by the whole thing.

I glanced out the window at the passing landscape as I tried to remove the image of Caleb digging up a grave from my mind. It was a gorgeous spring day. Sunny with a few wispy clouds against the blue, blue sky. The snow that had blanketed the ground for most of the winter had melted, leaving marshy green meadows with colorful wildflowers to enjoy. I tried hard to truly focus on the beauty, but all I could think about were the various scenarios for the crash and what each scenario might mean.

"If we set aside the idea of grave robbing for a moment and assume there were two people in the car before the crash and Caleb did manage to get out and someone else died, doesn't it seem that someone would be looking for the person who died? I mean, this person had a life before they died. Has anyone pulled missing person reports from around that time?"

"I haven't, but that's an excellent idea if we discover that Caleb is alive. If he actually did die in the accident, then looking for the identity of the actual victim of the crash is a mute theory."

I supposed Beck had a point. At this point, I supposed all we could do was keep an open mind as we tried to track down the man in the photo.

I glanced out the window again as we gained elevation. It really was pretty up this way. Since moving to Holiday Bay, I hadn't done much sightseeing in this area. Perhaps I'd see if Dawson wanted to dust off his Harley this weekend. The Bistro was closed on Sundays and Mondays until Memorial Day, and a meandering ride in the rural areas of Maine sounded like a relaxing way to spend a sunny spring day.

"I heard Sage is heading back to LA today," Beck said, changing the subject.

"Yeah. Sage decided that she'd hidden out in Maine long enough and truly needed to go home and sort out her life there. Her breakup with Scot was amenable, but I think there are still a lot of emotions at play. Scot moved out of the house they were sharing and left it to her, so she didn't have to deal with moving, but I imagine the space will feel pretty empty."

"I imagine it will, but at least she has a demanding career that will likely keep her distracted."

"She said almost the same thing. I know she has an awesome team at her LA facility, but even awesome employees need a bit of oversight. Sage has spent the majority of her time in Maine since November. I think Sage realizes that if she wants to keep what she has, she needs to pay some attention to it."

"From what I understand, it's actually her business and formal wear lines that gave her a name in the industry."

"It is," I agreed. "I'm not even sure why Sage decided to go all in on the outdoor and sport wear lines with Garret since it's her high-end clothing that makes her the money she has grown accustomed to."

"She seems to be integrating herself into the Holiday Bay culture."

"She has," I agreed. "And I will admit that Holiday Bay is the sort of place to lure you in and then capture your heart so that you'll never want to let go." I laughed. "When I came here for the first time after being summoned by my grandmother's attorney,

I really did plan to make the trip a quick in and quick out sort of thing, and yet here I am all these years later."

"Like I said, the place has a way of getting its hooks into you. Did Sage say when she'd be back?"

"Not for a few months, at the very least. Sage shared that she really did have a lot of work to catch up on, so she may not show up until the fall when things begin to gear up here with her winterwear launch."

"I guess her commitment to Garret allows her to spend time in both locations."

I nodded. "Garret really wanted Sage's creativity and eye for detail, so I know that when they sat down and worked out the details for their partnership in Sandy Dog Casual Beachwear, he was extremely accommodating to her needs."

Beck smiled. "I do love that name."

It suddenly occurred to me that his sandy dog, Meatball, wasn't with us, and I knew he hadn't brought him to the house for Dawson to watch while he was away, so I asked about him.

"He's with Lou and Toby today," Beck answered, referring to his friend and bookstore owner, Lou Prescott, and her rescue cat, Toby.

"It's nice that Meatball gets along with the cats who live in the bookstore."

"He's a good boy. Every now and then, I think about getting a second dog so he'll have company, but Meatball is an old dog who is fairly set in his ways. He likes who and what he likes, and I don't sense that he's looking to expand his social network much."

"He's an extremely patient dog. I see people stop by your booth all day who want to pet him and say hi, and he's always so polite and accommodating."

"Like I said, he's a good boy."

The conversation naturally stalled as we approached Sunday River. Beck suggested that we begin our search by having breakfast at a local café known as a favorite amongst residents. In addition to the photo Nell had provided of the dark-haired man at the music festival, Beck had also brought a recent photo of Caleb, which he found in his employee file. We hoped that someone in town would recognize one man or the other, and if one of the men was identified, then, hopefully, we could determine whether we had a match or not.

Chapter 4

The café was packed when we arrived, but two stools beside each other were available at the counter. We ordered coffee while we looked over the menu.

"Everything looks so good, but I want to keep it lite this morning. Maybe scrambled eggs, whole wheat toast, and fruit," I said.

"I'm going for the lumberjack special. It's a lot of food, but those flap jacks look too good to pass up."

I glanced at the menu. "Flapjacks, eggs, home fries, bacon, and sausage. That really is a big breakfast. I'd be sick all day if I ate that."

"The secret is pacing," Beck assured me.

When the waitress returned, Beck and I placed our order, and then I launched into my pre-prepared spiel. "Before you go, I wonder if you can help me," I said to the woman whose nametag indicated that her name was Lisa as I looked around. "I can see you're busy, so I'll only take a moment of your time."

"What do you need?" she asked.

I pulled out both photos and placed them on the counter. "I'm looking for a friend of mine. This is his employee photo," I pointed to the photo of Caleb that Beck had pulled from the town of Holiday Bay's website. "Do you recognize him?"

"No. Cute guy, but he doesn't look familiar."

I pointed to the dark-haired man in the image Nell had pulled off social media. "How about this man? This photo was taken here in Sunday River a couple weeks ago."

The woman picked the photo up and looked at it closely but denied having seen the man. She recognized the venue where the photo had been taken and suggested we speak with Marla. Apparently, Marla, who'd attended Spring Fling, was a long-time resident who seemed to know everyone. Marla was busy with a customer, but Lisa promised to send her over once she got freed up.

"This coffee is quite good," Beck said. "And only a buck for a bottomless cup."

"I can see why this place is so popular. The menu is extensive, the prices are very reasonable, and the food looks delicious. I'm not sure about the bottomless coffee promotion, however. Not that we don't serve bottomless coffee. Most places do. But there's already a line to get in, so I'd think they'd be trying to get folks to eat and move on rather than encouraging them to linger."

"I suppose there is a science to it. It always looks like you all do a good job keeping things moving at the Bistro."

"If it's busy, we clear the tables, provide checks, and wish our guests well to make it clear that as far as we're concerned, we're done. Of course, if it's slow and there isn't a line to get a table, we're fine with folks lingering. Discouraging folks from lingering while continuing to make them feel appreciated and welcome can be tricky to accomplish."

Beck looked over my shoulder. "It looks like Marla's on her way over."

I looked up and smiled at the middle-aged woman who was at least six feet tall and was as thin as she was tall.

"I understand you have a question for me."

Beck nodded and showed her the photos. She picked each one up and really took her time looking at them. "I don't recognize the man in what looks to be an employee photo, although he does look a lot like the man in the Spring Fling photo, who I also don't recognize. But I do recognize this woman." She pointed to a woman standing next to the man Nell thought might be Caleb at Spring Fling. "She's a local woman who goes by the name Heidi, but I think her real name is Gretchen."

"Do you know if Heidi was at the music festival with the dark-haired man?" Beck asked.

She shrugged. "I can't say that I know one way or another. I usually try to mind my own business. I imagine you can ask her if you want to know if she was with the guy or simply occupying the same physical space when the photo was taken."

"Do you have Heidi's contact information?" Beck asked.

"No. If you want that, you'll need to speak with Nan."

"Nan?"

"She owns the t-shirt shop two blocks over. Just turn right when you leave the restaurant, go down a block, make another right, and then a left at the first street you come to. You can't miss the place."

Beck thanked the woman and then offered her a compliment, which caused her to blush. Beck wasn't the sort to come on to every woman he met the way some men did, but there was something about his rugged good looks that had women his age taking a second look.

"So, do we head to the t-shirt shop?" I asked.

"We might as well."

Once I'd eaten most of my breakfast and Beck had polished off his, we headed to the t-shirt shop to ask Nan about the man in the photo. The woman said she didn't recognize him, but when we asked her if she knew how to contact Heidi, she informed us that

Heidi was out of town. Beck asked if she had a cell phone number, and Nan replied that she didn't, but she suggested that we speak with her sister, Gilly. If anyone had her cell phone number, it would be Gilly.

Once we finally made contact with Gilly, who Beck persuaded to provide us with Heidi's number, we called Heidi. She claimed that she'd been chatting with her friend, Faith, who had paused to talk to the guy when the photo was taken, but that she'd never actually spoken to him herself. She gave us Faith's number. And so it went. One clue led to the next, but no one claimed to recognize Caleb. If Caleb had been living in Sunday River for the past three months, then it seemed that someone would have recognized him. Wouldn't they?

"I think it's safe to say that even if the man in the photo is Caleb and he was here for Spring Fling a few weeks ago, he isn't here now. It's quite likely he was only passing through then," I said.

"I agree," Beck said. "It was worth checking out, but this is a small ski town. Everyone knows everyone. If Caleb had spent much time here, folks would recognize him."

"Maybe Dawson can clean up the photo that started this whole thing. Once he has a clear photo, he can run it through his facial recognition program. If we can prove that the man in the photo isn't Caleb with any degree of certainty, we'll have solved at least part of the puzzle."

"That's a good idea," Beck said. "I need to stop for gas, and then we'll head home."

I decided to take advantage of the fact that Beck had stopped at a gas station with a decent-looking mini-mart to use the restroom.

"Can I help you?" the kid behind the counter asked.

"Restrooms?"

"Back of the store to the left."

I thanked the guy and then headed to take care of what needed taking care of. On my way out to meet back up with Beck, I decided to show the photo of the dark-haired man taken at the Spring Fling to the kid. It was a long shot, but I had a copy of the photo in my purse, and since Beck was still messing around at the pump, I figured I had a moment or two.

"Would you mind looking at this for me?" I asked the kid, who looked to be around nineteen or twenty.

He shrugged.

I slid the photo across the counter. "Do you recognize this man?" I pointed to the dark-haired man.

"Yeah, I know him," the kid responded. "His name is Hogan. He's a roadie for the band."

"Do you have a last name?" I asked.

He shook his head. "Why are you asking? Is Hogan in trouble?"

"No, Hogan isn't in trouble. I'm actually in town looking for someone with a similar look." I slid Caleb's employee photo across the counter. "This man."

The kid stared at the photo. "I guess this guy does look like Hogan, but the guy I met wasn't nearly as polished and put together as this other guy."

"The second photo is an employee photo, so it's a bit more formal. Do you know if Hogan is still in town?" I asked, figuring it would be best to speak with the man ourselves.

"He's not. Like I said, he was with the band. He left when they did."

"You wouldn't happen to know how long Hogan has been traveling with the band, would you?"

He shrugged. "I'm not sure. He never really said. We only chatted for a few minutes. The band stopped for fuel, junk food, and a bathroom break on the way into town, and while they were here, I chatted with a few of the guys."

"Do you know where the band was heading next?"

"Sorry. I have no idea."

I gave the kid some cash for the information he provided and then headed back to Beck's truck. When we were both settled in the truck, I shared my conversation with the clerk with Beck. "So what do you think?"

Beck answered. "I think that if the kid working in the convenience store thinks there is even a possibility that Caleb and Hogan might be the same person, we need to track down Hogan. It shouldn't be all that difficult to find out where the band headed after they left here. In fact, why don't you call Dawson and ask him to see what he can find out."

I agreed to make the call, and Dawson was happy to help. He called back a few minutes later to tell us that the band had a gig in Vermont this weekend and was likely headed in that direction. Beck suggested that Dawson try to get contact information for one of the band members, which Dawson agreed to do. He said he'd find out what he could and call us back.

"So, do you plan on telling Nell what we've discovered so far?" I asked.

"No, at least not yet, because in my mind, it's still a long shot that Caleb and Hogan are the same guy. All we have to go on is a grainy photo and the statement from a man who spoke to the band for a few minutes that the guy in the employee photo somewhat looked like the guy with the band. If Caleb was traveling with the band as Hogan, I'll track him down, and we'll take it from there."

I glanced out the window just in time to see a large hawk land on a fence parallelling the road. There were a ton of hawks in the area, so seeing one wasn't all that unusual, but there was just something about how this particular bird looked at me.

"Do you believe in spirit animals?" I asked Beck.

"Spirit animals? Do you mean animals who bring a message with their appearance?"

"I guess. I don't know much about this sort of thing, but Nikki is really into it and talks about it quite a lot, and she made some statements that got me thinking."

"Thinking?"

"Thinking about messages from the spirit world, I guess. I don't know what I mean exactly. Nikki says that visits from a hawk can indicate that I should listen to my intuition and not let myself get distracted, but that seemed pretty vague, and I really had no way of giving her statement much context. Still..."

"Still?"

"It's just that I've seen a lot of hawks lately. And not just in a casual way, like a hawk up a tree or sitting on the roof. But meaningful encounters, such as waking to find a hawk looking in my bedroom window and having a hawk land on the back of the chair across from me when I was sitting on the rooftop doing paperwork the other day. I even had a hawk land on a log where I'd paused to get the sand out of my shoe while walking with Goliath on the beach across from the Bistro, and just now, a hawk landed on the fence that runs along the highway, and when we passed, he really looked at me."

"And you think this hawk has a message for you?" Beck asked.

Did I think that? "I don't know. Maybe. Probably not. While I realize this may sound peculiar, the encounters have been odd." I turned slightly in my seat so that I faced Beck. "So what do you think? Are spirit animals even a possibility?"

"There are more things on Heaven and earth, Horatio, than are dreamt of in your philosophy."

"Shakespeare," I said.

He nodded. "I don't know if your hawk encounters are meaningful, but to me, it seems that the answer to that question is one only you can know."

I supposed Beck was right. If the hawk had been trying to communicate with me, then the message he'd been trying to share was one only I could know.

When we returned to the Bistro, Beck headed into the bar to talk to Dawson, but I noticed that Holiday Bay's newest resident, Kyle Young, and his friend, Kelly, were having dinner in the dining room. Kyle had recently taken a job with the town as the official IT guy, and it suddenly occurred to me that he must have been hired to take over for Caleb after he died. Holiday Bay was a small town, and there was no way there were two employees with the same role.

After deciding to stop and chat with him, I headed in that direction.

"Hey, guys," I greeted the pair.

"Hey, Shelby," Kyle replied. "I didn't notice that you were here."

"I actually just arrived. I apologize for interrupting your dinner date, but I would really appreciate it if I could speak with you about Caleb Farmer."

"The man I replaced?"

I confirmed that the man Kyle referred to was the person who had been on my mind.

"What about him?" Kyle asked.

"I'm not sure if you've heard, but Beck was hired by Caleb's sister to look into the accident that ended his life."

"I guess Beck did mention something about that. He called me late in the afternoon yesterday and asked me if I had access to items left behind by Caleb, such as his computer, desk calendar, notes, files, and that sort of thing. I told him that I had a few things, such as work files and his computer, but that someone had cleaned out Caleb's personal possessions after his death."

"I heard his car blew up, and there was basically nothing left," Kelly jumped into the conversation.

"That's what I heard as well," I said. "I know figuring out what happened to Caleb isn't Beck's job, and it certainly isn't mine, but I've spent time with Beck chasing down a few recent leads, so I guess it would be accurate to say that I'm curious."

"I guess I'm curious, too," Kyle admitted. "Do you think this man's death had anything to do with his job? Might it have been something more than an accident?"

"Probably not," I assured him. I supposed just asking these questions might have caused feelings of panic. "It's just that I thought that things like desk calendars and phone logs might provide information about what happened during his final days."

Kyle smiled. "I'm sorry to inform you, but no one with any level of comfort with computers, the internet, and computer software would use a desk calendar or phone log. At least not a paper desk calendar or phone log. If you are determined to find out what the man was doing during his final hours, what you need to do is log into his cloud account. I assume the detective who investigated the accident has already done that."

I suspected that was likely true. I supposed I could ask Beck about it.

"There is one thing I might know," Kyle said. "I don't know if this is anything, but I've been getting strange emails directed to Caleb every Tuesday. The emails don't make sense to me, and I suspect the content is personal, but there's no way to reply to the email to let the sender know that Caleb has passed away."

"And the emails? What sort of content are we talking about?"

"The email is a single line of text written as a series of names and numbers. The names and numbers vary each week, but the overall text is something like: 'Charlie fifteen, Hector twenty-five, Oliver three, Mike nine, and Paul three.'"

"So what do you think the messages are all about?" I asked. "Some sort of passcode?"

Kyle shrugged. "A passcode is a good guess. My line of work requires me to be involved with multiple passcodes, but if these are passcodes, they aren't the same as others I've seen. I can forward the emails to Beck if you think that would help."

"Forward them to Dawson. I'll text you his email address. In the meantime, look around. You may actually know something that you don't even realize that you know. Or maybe you have something you don't even know you have."

"Have something?"

"A secret file, for example," I suggested. "It could even be a file hidden on the man's computer. Or perhaps there's a secret email account or a key hidden in a desk drawer that might open a safety deposit box. I know I'm basically just making stuff up at this point, but the reality is that since you have access to his office and computer, you could have access to the very clue we need to solve this case, and you don't even know it."

"I suddenly feel like I've landed in a James Bond movie."

I supposed the nature of Caleb's death did make it appear like there was espionage of some sort at hand.

I turned my attention to Kelly. "I'm going to grab your drinks, which will be on the house, and then I want to hear about your new job."

"I haven't started it yet, but I'm happy to tell you about it."

"Haven't started it yet? I thought you got a waitstaff job at the Cliff House."

"I thought so as well, but then they decided they didn't want to hire any new personnel until after the remodel, which isn't set to wrap up until the end of May. I needed some income, so I accepted a temporary nanny position, but that job concluded a week ago. I was back to scanning through the help wanted ads when I ran into Cricket Abernathy. She told me about a potential job opportunity working for a group of women who had recently opened a wellness center near the flower shop. She asked if I'd like her to introduce us, and I said I would. The place is awesome, and the new owners are the coolest people I've ever met."

"Hold that thought. I want to hear all about it," I said as I headed to the bar to grab the drinks. Nikki had just dropped off empties from another table, so I sent her to take their food order. Once I returned to the table, I asked Kelly about her new job.

"So tell me about this new enterprise."

"The name of the new place is Elevate."

"Interesting name."

"Their mission statement is to transcend your limitations by elevating your mind, body, and spirit. The three women who run the place have a holistic approach to life."

"Okay. Then tell me about the three women who run the place. How are they qualified to help us mere mortals ascend to the next level?"

Kelly smiled. "I can tell you're skeptical, but give it a try. I promise this place is like nothing you've ever experienced."

"Okay, I'm keeping an open mind."

"A woman named Gaia was the one to actually hire me. She seems to focus on health and relaxation through bodywork and movement. Not only does she offer a wide variety of spa-type services, such as massages, but she also has a background in Chinese medicine and is a certified acupuncturist. In addition to bodywork on the table, she offers classes focused on mindful movement, such as yoga and tai chi."

"Is Gaia petite with long white hair and a sort of ageless quality that causes you to wonder how old she really is?"

Kelly confirmed that was the case. "Why do you ask? Have you met her?"

"No, but I did see a woman who fits that description doing tai chi on the beach during sunrise a couple of weeks ago when Dawson and I had decided to take an early morning run. The woman appeared to be making the movements without any effort being extended, as if she was working in a gravity-free environment. It was beautiful. Dawson and I paused to watch for a moment, but we couldn't decide how old the woman was."

"I think she's in her sixties, although I've never asked her about it since it didn't seem to be any of my business."

"Understood. And the other women you mentioned who work with Gaia."

"Kai is into the whole mind/body thing. She's probably in her thirties and is a licensed therapist with a doctorate in counseling. What makes what she does unique is her approach. Instead of interview style therapy where the counselor sits in a chair, and the patient sits on a sofa across from her, Kai utilizes techniques such as meditation, movement, art therapy, and hypnosis."

"So she never uses talk therapy?" I asked.

"Based on what I know at this point, she will use talk therapy when she feels that's the best course of action for the specific client she's working with but truly prefers to get the entire mind and body involved."

"That sounds interesting. And the third co-owner? I think I remember you mentioning that there were three."

She nodded. "Serena is a naturopath. She seems to know all about the herbs, lotions, and supplements that are sold onsite. This is an area I'm not familiar with, but I'm excited to learn."

"It does sound like an amazing place to work."

"I think it will be. The first time I walked into the space, I felt the tension melt from my body. The moment you walk in the door, it feels as if a serene energy envelopes you. You really do need to stop by when you can."

"I will. And what job will you be doing exactly?"

"I initially applied for work as a masseuse since I worked as a licensed masseuse before I abandoned my old life and unwisely followed a guy to Maine. But they don't need another masseuse at this point. Gaia said that she enjoyed my energy and would talk things over with Kai and Serena, and after a bit of back and forth, it was decided that they would train me to work the front desk. I'll deal with the sale of herbal remedies, appointments, inventory, and that sort of thing."

"It does sound pretty great, and as you suggested, I'll need to check it out."

"I'm starting next week, although all I will be doing for the first month is training."

I wished I could stay and chat longer, but I had a business to run, so I said my goodbyes and promised to keep in touch. I headed to the bar to let Dawson know about the emails Kyle would be forwarding to him.

Chapter 5

By the time Friday rolled around, Beck had been able to track down the band the man who looked like Caleb had been seen with. The band member Beck spoke to confirmed that Hogan had only been traveling with them for a couple months, and while he was a good worker, he tended to be skittish. Beck hoped to obtain contact information for the man known as Hogan but was told that Hogan decided to part ways with the band after Sunday River and hadn't even come by to collect his last check. Beck and Dawson had compared notes and decided to look for Caleb using Dawson's facial recognition software. They hadn't gotten a hit yet, but Dawson had been working on the emails Kyle forwarded to him. Over coffee that morning, Dawson indicated that he may have determined a motive for Caleb to merely disappear.

"Go on," I persuaded, even though I had lots to do today.

"It looks as if the emails Kyle intercepted came from CHOMP," Dawson said.

"Chomp?" I asked as I poured myself a cup of coffee.

Dawson nodded. "All caps. I've heard about this." He entered a series of commands. "Based on what I've heard, CHOMP is a secret online betting site and only open to members."

"And how do you become a member?" I asked.

"You have to be referred by someone," Dawson answered. "I'm not the type to want to engage in this sort of activity, so I haven't looked into it, but based on what I've heard, the membership requires some sort of huge buy-in, and those who are members seem to have been hand-selected."

"So, how does it work?"

Dawson frowned as he did a quick search on his computer. "I'm not sure exactly. I assume the members are given a link to access the betting site. And to me, the weekly emails Caleb has been receiving seem to contain the passcode to access that week's game or games. If Caleb's account is still funded, then the computer that runs the whole thing likely doesn't know that he's no longer active and has continued to send the codes. Since having a complete understanding of how all this works is necessary, it seems digging around a little more will be required." Dawson typed in a few more commands.

"Okay," I said. "So let me see if I understand this. CHOMP is an illegal online betting site with an exclusive membership. I'm going to assume the stakes are high, and while it likely takes a good amount of cash to play, if you win, the payouts are substantial."

"I would agree with that assessment," Dawson said.

"How are the bets funded?" I asked. "Credit card? Prepaid account? Cash app of some sort?"

Dawson answered. "As best as I can tell, when you set up an account, you also set up a cash account. A cash app is linked to a bank account, which funds the cash account. You then use the cash in this account for the weekly buy-in. If you win, the cash is deposited into this same account. You can then use your cash for bets and buy-ins in future weeks, or if you choose, you can eventually cash out, and the cash in the account will be transferred to the same bank account used to fund the game account in the first place. There may be more to it, but I think that's the gist of it. I plan to dig around a bit more to see if I'm missing something, but I'm guessing that Caleb may have chosen to disappear if he happened to get in too deep."

That seemed to make sense. "Keep me in the loop."

"I will." Dawson looked toward the countertop at the back of the room piled high with boxes. "It looks as if Amy has been packing."

"She has. I think she hopes to move this weekend."

Dawson smiled. "And then we'll have the house to ourselves."

"We will," I confirmed. I'd begun to have mixed feelings about the fact that it would just be Dawson and me in my huge house. I wasn't sure why. I was happy with the way things were going with our relationship, but now that Dawson had confirmed the couple wanted to lease his house, there was no denying the fact that we were actually living together. As long as he had his own place, and I had mine, I could tell myself that we weren't actually living together. But now...

The only man, other than Dawson, I'd ever lived with was Scot, and that arrangement had come about in a very different manner than the cohabitation situation with Dawson. Scot and I began as friends, and when he'd needed a place to crash, I'd invited him to sleep on my sofa, which eventually led to him sleeping in my bed, and we'd morphed from friends into lovers from that point. There had never been a plan to date, and there absolutely had never been a plan to cohabitate as a committed couple. It all seemed to happen organically. One day, we'd been friends, and then, suddenly, we were lovers, but it seemed to work.

With Dawson, the road from friendship to romance had been very different. For one thing, we'd taken things ridiculously slow. For another, we tended to think about and discuss every step along the way, so every decision was calculated and well thought out. I guessed that rather than "falling" in love, we carefully navigated the course, and at some point, we'd decided to be in love. Not that our carefully planned out route was a problem since, in the end, I did love Dawson and was thrilled to have him in my life. But our carefully navigated course did require that Dawson and I take ownership of where we were in our relationship and where we were going.

I supposed that allowing ourselves to be swept along in a current with no predetermined direction, like I'd done with Scot, would have been easier. But in the end, easier with Scot hadn't been better. What I had with Dawson was definitely more complicated, but I hoped that the well-thought-out path we seemed to be traveling would lead to a "happily ever after" for both of us.

"Is something on your mind?" Dawson asked.

"No, I just have a lot to do today. I'm going to hop in the shower. I know you don't start until two, but I think I'll head in early today."

"Okay," Dawson kissed me on the lips. "I think I'll work on this CHOMP thing some more. I'll see you this afternoon."

Once I arrived at the Bistro, I headed upstairs to my office. There was nothing like bookkeeping to distract my mind from all the changes in my life.

Nikki stuck her head in my office through the open door several hours later. "Abby and Georgia are downstairs having lunch if you want to come down and say hi."

"Thanks for letting me know. I definitely want to say hi," I said, pushing back from my desk where I'd been inputting expenses into my accounting program. "And I could really use a break. I feel like I've been tied to this desk for hours."

"Actually, it has been hours," Nikki said. "It's not good for your body to sit so long. You need to get up and stretch."

I knew Nikki was right, but occasionally, it was challenging to identify a natural place to take a break.

"You said come down," I clarified. "Abby and Georgia aren't on the rooftop? Today is opening day for the season."

"It's raining. No one is on the rooftop."

I frowned. "Really? It was sunny when I arrived."

Nikki chuckled. "Like I said, that was hours ago. Go ahead and finish what you're doing. I'll tell Abby and Georgia that you'll be right down. They were just seated before I came up, so it will be a while before they're ready to leave."

As it turned out, Nikki had interrupted me at a pretty good stopping point, so I saved my work and logged off. I stopped by the ladies' room to freshen up and then headed downstairs, where Abby and Georgia had been seated at a four-top in front of the large picture window in the bar. Dawson had arrived for his shift, but then he and Beck had gone off somewhere together, so except for Abby and Georgia, the bar was currently empty.

"It really is raining," I said as I slid onto a chair at their table.

"It has been for a couple hours," Georgia said.

"I had no idea. It was sunny when I arrived at the Bistro and headed up to my office to deal with the accounting that I seem to always be months behind on. I lost track of time and haven't taken a break since I've been here. I was delighted when Nikki poked her head into my office to tell me you were here." I glanced at the clock. It was already two o'clock. "So, what are the two of you up to?" I asked.

"I needed to come into town to check out the kitchen Brad arranged for my use for the cooking specials I'll be taping in a few weeks," Georgia said, referring to Brad Kingman, the owner of the cable television station she worked for.

"I heard that you would be filming eight episodes in a single week. Whose kitchen are you using?"

"We're actually using the kitchen at the Cliff House," Georgia informed me.

"I thought they were renovating the restaurant." I remembered that Kelly had mentioned the renovation the Cliff House was undergoing as the reason she wasn't working there.

"I guess they plan to be closed for six weeks to renovate the dining room and won't need to use the kitchen. The kitchen isn't part of the project, which is cosmetic in nature, so Brad worked it out so that I could use the kitchen during the evenings. There will be noise from the renovation between eight and five, so I plan to meet my film crew at Cliff House at six each evening. I'll do all the prep work that won't be filmed at home so we can film a segment in a couple hours. I'm hoping to be home by eleven at the latest. I must admit that working so late in the evening isn't my first choice, but the Cliff House has a beautiful kitchen. I think it will provide a perfect backdrop for my series."

"And why didn't you just use the kitchen in the inn?" I wondered.

"Filming eight segments at the inn would have been disruptive to the guests now that we've reopened after our remodel following the flood in the basement. Using a commercial kitchen with room for a full film crew was the only option outside of driving to the studio in Bangor each day and using the kitchen there, which, as you know, I really didn't want to do."

Nikki brought the salads the women had ordered and then sat on the fourth chair. The lunch crowd had thinned down to a few diners in the dining room, so I supposed she had a moment to sit and chat with her sister-in-law. "I hate to interrupt your conversation, but a couple was in earlier, and the husband asked about Rosalyn." Rosalyn Montgomery had been our dining room manager for a short time after our long-time dining room manager, Kennedy Swanson, had moved out of the area. "I told him that she'd decided to take a job she'd been offered in San Francisco, and he asked about a replacement. I told him that Rosalyn had only recently left and that we hadn't gotten around to hiring anyone new, and he wondered if we'd be willing to interview his granddaughter."

"Does this granddaughter have any experience managing a dining room?" I asked.

"I asked that very question," Nikki confirmed. "I guess she was the assistant manager of a seafood restaurant in Florida until she moved to Maine to help her grandparents so that they could remain independent for as long as possible. According to the man, before the granddaughter agreed to move in with them, he and his wife had been looking at assisted living as their only option. But with the granddaughter to help with specific activities, such as driving, shopping, snow removal, and heavy cleaning, they expect to be able to spend at least a few more years in the home they love."

I couldn't help but admire the granddaughter for giving up her life to help her grandparents, but it sounded like taking care of them might already be a full-time job. I said as much.

"All the guy was asking for was an interview." Nikki handed me a piece of paper with a name and phone number. "If you want to call and speak with Harlee, here's her number."

I accepted the paper and promised to call and talk to the granddaughter. I couldn't promise anything, but I had to admire the woman and was willing to at least speak with her. Once she'd delivered the note, Nikki left to cash out her last customer from the lunch crowd. There would be a lull before the bar and dinner crowd began to arrive, which is when the staff took a break and did any clean-up that we needed to do.

I turned my attention back toward Abby and Georgia. "Dealing with employee management is the hardest part of this job."

"It is," Georgia agreed. "Getting the right person settled in the right job is very important."

I thought about Rosalyn. She'd been the most qualified employee I'd ever had, but she never really fit into the Bistro's family like Kennedy had.

"Georgia and I have hired a bunch of random people along the way who weren't necessarily qualified for the job we hired them to perform at the time we hired them, but in the end, they turned out to be exactly the sort of people we needed," Abby said.

"I get that," I agreed. "And I'm not averse to training the right person. We do need a dining room manager, and after working with Rosalyn, who was very qualified but not quite the right fit in terms of personality, I know how important it is to find someone who fits in with our existing family."

"How has it been working since Rosalyn left?" Abby asked.

"We seem to be doing fine with the staff we have, but it is still the off-season. Once summer hits, I'll need someone on the floor who can make decisions and handle conflicts. Someone who will be willing to get to know the customers, is willing to work with the staff, and is firm but flexible at the same time. Someone like Kennedy."

"Kennedy leaving was a tough blow, but it sounds as if she made the best decision for Addy," Georgia referred to Kennedy's genius daughter, who had enrolled in a school for gifted students.

"I chat with Kennedy at least every few weeks, and she assures me that Addy is thriving and there is no doubt in her mind that she made the right decision."

"I'm so happy to hear that," Abby said.

Beck came in with Meatball and headed directly to his booth. He sat down, pulled a file out, opened it for a quick review, looked at his cell phone, picked up the file, and headed back the way he came.

"I guess he must be working on a case," I said.

"Looked like it," Georgia agreed. "Speaking of cases, I heard he was looking into Caleb Farmer's accident."

"Caleb's sister, Nell, hired him to look into things after she saw a photo of a man she thought might be her brother that was taken at a music festival after he died and was posted online. Did you know Caleb?"

"Sort of. Tanner needed some help with a change in county ordinances, and he asked Caleb to walk him through a few things. I guess that was maybe a year ago. Then, a few months after that, we ran into Caleb and his girlfriend at one of the community events in the park. I forget which one, but it was this past summer. We started chatting, and Tanner invited Caleb and his girl to have dinner with us. Tanner wanted to pay him back for his help, so we took them to the Cliff House. It would be fair to say I got to know Caleb and Tamara somewhat well during the meal. I wouldn't say well, but Tanner is a pro at asking the right questions to get people talking."

"Are you talking about Tamara Colefort?"

"Yes. Do you know Tamara?"

"She comes in from time to time. I don't know her well, but she seems like a nice woman."

"She really seemed to be, and we had a lovely evening. When I heard that Caleb had died in a horrible car accident, I felt so bad. I wanted to send flowers to his funeral but hadn't heard about one, so I asked Tamara. She told me that she and Caleb had broken up a month or so before he died and wasn't being kept in the loop when it came to things like funerals."

"I'm sorry to hear that," I said. "Breakups are always hard, but then to have your ex die in such a horrible way must really compound things."

"Tamara was pretty broken up when I spoke to her. I had the feeling that the breakup was pretty messy. She didn't go into detail, but it sounded as if Caleb had gotten into financial trouble and had apparently turned to extreme measures to get himself out of it. Tamara said that toward the end, Caleb really changed, but not in a good way."

The words financial trouble combined with extreme measures, had me thinking about a strong motive for someone to fake their death. At this point, I didn't say so, but I would say something to Beck once he returned from wherever he'd gone.

"Listen to that." I turned and looked out the window as the sound of sirens intensified. "It sounds like the entire police force is heading somewhere."

"I wonder what's going on," Georgia stated.

Abby grabbed her cell phone. "Colt is likely tied up. I'll call Gabby and see what I can find out."

Colt Wilder was both the chief of police and Abby's boyfriend, and Gabby Gibson was Colt's receptionist and dispatcher. If anyone could find out what was going on, Abby could.

"Hey, Gabby," I watched as she connected with the police dispatcher. "Georgia and I are in town and can hear the sirens. What's going on?"

I couldn't hear Gabby's reply, but based on the look on Abby's face, something pretty bad was going on.

"Wow. That is so hard to believe. I know you're busy, so I won't keep you. Thanks for the update." Abby hung up.

"What happened?" I asked.

"Gavin Houghton was found dead."

"Oh no," Georgia said. "What happened?"

"Gabby didn't know a lot," Abby answered. "She just said that Gavin didn't show up for work today and didn't call in. He missed an important meeting with a developer that his staff didn't think he'd willingly miss, so they were worried when he didn't show up. They began calling around and eventually called Colt to report Gavin as missing. His body was found behind the dunes that run between the low point in the shoreline out near Sunrise Beach and the highway. Gabby wasn't sure about the cause of death or anything else at this point."

I informed the women that Sunrise Beach was just down the road from the condo Amy and Cambria were moving into.

"Amy and Cambria are moving into a condo?" Georgia asked.

I briefly filled her in.

"Those are nice condos," Georgia said. "I heard that unless you're lucky enough to know someone, it's almost impossible to get one of those units since they rent out as soon as they're listed."

"It sounds like they were in the right place at the right time," I responded.

Nikki and Charmaine both came into the bar. "Did you hear?" Nikki asked.

"We did," I verified.

"Lucy just showed up for her late shift and told me that her friend from the psychology class she's taking at the college lives in those apartments just east of the beach near the dunes."

"The Surfside," I said, picturing the light blue building.

"I think that might be it," Nikki confirmed. "It's that building that faces the dunes, not the condos across from the beach."

"I think that's the Surfside," Georgia confirmed. "So, did you have a point about Lucy's friend?"

"Oh yeah. Anyway, Lucy called her friend, and the friend told Lucy that the local and state police were at what she assumed must be a crime scene since they blocked off the road in both directions."

"Where is Lucy?" I asked, looking around. If Lucy had just arrived, I would have thought she would have been the one telling the story rather than Nikki.

"She went upstairs to return a cookbook she'd borrowed from Amy," Charmaine informed us. "I imagine she's filling Amy and Cambria in right now."

"Charmaine and I asked around, and it sounds like the body of our town manager was found not all that far from the condos they're moving into, so I'm sure they'll be interested in the news," Nikki said.

It did sound as if that might be the case. "Do we have any customers left in the dining room?" I asked.

Nikki informed me that everyone had left, so other than Abby and Georgia, just staff was onsite.

Amy, Cambria, and Lucy wandered into the bar a few minutes later. "Any news about Gavin Houghton?" Amy asked.

Abby shared what she knew with the new arrivals, which wasn't a lot, but the share did lead to a rather lengthy discussion. The discussion was based more on supposition than fact since no one had the facts, but it kept us busy for the next hour. By the time the conversation wrapped up, Abby and Georgia announced that they needed to head back to the inn, but they promised to text us if they got any updates. After they departed, the five of us still at the Bistro moved over to a larger table near the front of the bar and restaurant, where we could keep an eye on the front door. None of us knew what had happened, but everyone had a theory they hadn't yet had the chance to share, which kept us busy until Beck showed up with an actual update.

Chapter 6

Beck had a date with his good friend, Lou Prescott, so he left shortly after dropping something off for Dawson. I, of course, had asked him if he had any news about Gavin Houghton before he left, and all he said was that it appeared that someone had bludgeoned him with a cylindrical shaped object, wrapped him in a rug, and then dumped him from a moving vehicle. Beck thought it odd that the killer would move the body only to dump him on a highway where he would assuredly be found. If the reason for moving the body wasn't to conceal it, what was the reason for relocating it?

I asked Beck if he knew where Houghton had actually died, and he said that as far as he knew, the police had not as of yet discovered the scene of the murder. I thought about sharing the details of my discussion with Georgia and Abby but decided to wait until the following day since we really did seem busy.

As expected, the bar was packed with locals trying to get an update on the newest crisis to strike our small town. I'd called and spoken to Alex, hoping she'd have an official update to offset some of the gossip, but she said they didn't know much more about what had occurred than I did at this point. Houghton was last seen leaving the town offices yesterday afternoon. He hadn't said where he'd been going, only that he likely wouldn't be back. Since Houghton had logged out of his computer and secured his office for the day, there was no immediate cause for concern regarding his absence until the man didn't appear at the meeting he'd scheduled this morning. Houghton's secretary had called him, but he hadn't answered. At this point, folks were concerned but still weren't overly worried. And then a motorist on the road just happened to see something reflecting off the sun down in the ditch at the base of the dunes and stopped to check it out. It was this motorist who found Houghton's body.

"What can I get you guys?" I asked a group of four lobstermen who'd wandered in after a long day on the water. Being as close to the commercial marina as the Bistro was, the men and women who worked the fishing boats for a living were generally our best customers.

"Pitcher and a basket," one of the men everyone called Gilligan replied.

"Hot, mild, teriyaki, or barbecue?" I asked about the wings I knew Gilligan had requested when he'd asked for a basket.

"Half hot and half barbecue. And toss in some fries. Have you seen Trawler?"

"Not yet," I replied. "There's still a large table in the back if you want to grab it. It'll seat six, so if Hook and Trawler show up, they can join you."

Gilligan thanked me and then headed toward the back of the room. I filled a pitcher with the dark stuff I knew Gilligan and his friends preferred and then dropped it off at the table with some glasses before sending the wing order to the kitchen. As I passed a table occupied by a group who looked to be teachers from the high school, I paused to ask them if Nikki had taken their order or if they still needed to order.

"Nikki took our order," a man in a dark blue polo shirt replied. "She went to the kitchen to see if any ribs from the lunch menu were left."

I guessed I did notice that Amy had ribs and fries on special during the lunch hour.

"So, what have you heard about Houghton?" a woman in a purple sweater asked.

"Not much," I replied. "It sounds like the man met with foul play, but I really don't know much beyond that."

"I heard that Colt hauled that ex-con Alex and Leo have working for them in for questioning," a man I knew as Skip commented.

"Colt arrested Cayson?" I asked.

The man nodded. "That's what I heard, although, in all fairness, the word arrested wasn't used during the conversation I overheard."

"I'm not surprised," the woman in the purple sweater said. "You let those folks live in your community, and you should expect trouble. I mean, the man already killed once. It's no big surprise that he'd likely kill again."

"I knew that man was trouble the minute he stepped foot in this town," the man in the dark blue polo said.

My instinct was to stick up for Cayson, but since I didn't have any facts, anything I said would merely be argumentative, so I held my tongue for now. I was going to head upstairs to check in with Nikki, but then I noticed her coming down the stairs with a platter overflowing with ribs and fries. I supposed that would satisfy the group for the time being.

As I walked away, the woman sitting next to Skip commented about Cayson getting back at Houghton for trying to block Leo from hiring him in the first place. It was true that Houghton had been vocal about Leo's choice of contractor and had even threatened to pull Leo's permit at one point if he didn't reconsider his choice; however, since the facility Alex and Leo were in the process of building was on county land and not within the town limits, there wasn't much Houghton, as town manager, could do to stop Leo from hiring whomever he wanted.

"Are you ready to order?" I asked a young couple I didn't recognize.

"We're actually waiting for some friends," the woman answered. "Maybe I'll just start with a glass of wine while we wait."

I asked the woman which of the many fine wines that we carried she'd like to try, and then I recited the beers on tap for the man she was with. Since their friends still hadn't arrived when I delivered their beverages, I asked the couple if they'd like to start with an appetizer while they waited. The woman responded that an order of crab cakes or possibly wontons might be a good idea. The man she was with asked about an appetizer menu, which I handed him. He passed the menu to the woman he was with.

"Has Jim texted you back?" the woman asked the man as she considered the appetizer menu.

"I haven't heard from him since he texted to let me know he needed to head to the police station to give a statement before he could meet us," the man said.

The woman looked up from the menu she'd been perusing. "Our friend, Jim, was the one who found that body on the side of the highway."

"Really," I said. "I heard that a body had been found, but I never did get any of the details." I decided to play it low-key in the hope the woman knew more about the situation and would be motivated to continue to share what she knew.

"This totally dead guy was wrapped in a rug and dumped down by the dunes. Hoyt and I don't live here in the area, so we aren't familiar with the specifics, but our friend, Jim, and his wife, Jessica, live in town. I called Jessica after Jim texted Hoyt, and she told me that the guy worked for the town. I guess he was the head guy or one of the head guys. Anyway, Jessica told me that this guy had his head smashed in before he was wrapped in a hideous checkerboard rug and tossed into the ditch like a piece of garbage."

I wrinkled my nose. Bludgeoning as a cause of death had been mentioned, but somehow, the woman who was sharing her news made the whole thing sound a lot more graphic.

"I guess we'll take the crab stuffed chili relleno and the crab cakes," the woman announced. "There's no telling how long our friends will be, and I'm starving."

"I wanted the chicken wings," Hoyt said.

"We have an appetizer sampler," I informed the pair. "You can pick four appetizers to share."

"That sounds good." Hoyt looked at his date. "The crab stuffed chili relleno, crab cakes, chicken wings, and what else?"

"The wontons. They do sound interesting."

I sent the order up to the kitchen and then headed to the bar to see if Dawson had heard anything new about Houghton's murder. The regulars, who usually lined up along the bar each evening after getting off work, usually had the inside scoop on what was happening even when no one else did.

"Any updates on Houghton?" I asked Dawson as he shook vodka and ice for a martini.

"I have heard a few things, but none of what I've heard has been verified."

"From a reliable source?"

"If you consider JJ a reliable source."

I knew that by saying JJ, he likely meant John Jensen Jones, a local handyman and day laborer who tended to migrate from job to job, never settling anywhere for long.

"What did JJ have to say?" I asked.

"He said that Houghton and Cayson got into it big time yesterday after Houghton showed up on the job site Leo hired Cayson to oversee."

I frowned. "Did the altercation get physical?"

"JJ says no. He mentioned that the crew had been steadily working to meet the daily goal when Houghton showed up at the job site. Cayson walked over to Houghton's car to speak with him, and JJ said that while he couldn't really hear much of what was being said, the exchange got ugly. Houghton got out of the car and tried to give something to Cayson. A piece of paper. Cayson balled up the paper, tossed it on the ground, and poked a finger into Houghton's chest. Houghton kicked dirt on Cayson's shoes, picked up the wadded-up piece of paper he'd tried to give Cayson, got into his car, and left. JJ said that

Flick Paulson is also working on the dog rescue crew, and after Houghton left, Paulson pulled Cayson aside and said something to him, and then Cayson left. JJ said he didn't come back the rest of the day."

"Did JJ think Cayson followed Houghton and then killed him?" I asked. I could see how folks in town who didn't think Cayson should be allowed to be part of our community would go there.

"JJ said that he didn't know, but he also said that Cayson was madder than he'd ever seen him after Houghton handed him the paper he brought out to deliver."

"But JJ didn't know what was on the paper?"

"He said he didn't."

When I noticed that the couple I'd ordered appetizers for had been joined by their friends, I headed over to take Jim and Jessica's drink order. I didn't know the couple well, but I had spoken with them occasionally when they'd come in for a meal. I hoped the group would be talking about Houghton, but instead, they ordered both drinks and their meals and then launched into a conversation about the concert on the beach they planned to head to after they ate. I was tempted to bring the discovery of Houghton's body up myself, but since they hadn't broached the subject, I decided it would be impolite for me to do so. I went up to the kitchen to grab the appetizer tray that had already been ordered, gave Amy the dinner order the four had put in, grabbed the beverages Jim and Jessica had ordered, and headed back toward the table where the topic of conversation was the hideous haircut a mutual friend had just gotten.

"Your dinners should be down shortly. Is there anything else I can get you for now?"

"I think we're good," Jim said. "Say Shelby, I know you've lived in town for a while, and I was wondering if you knew which hotel the blue and pink checkerboard rug Gavin Houghton's body was found wrapped in might have come from."

"Blue and pink checkerboard? Are you sure it came from a hotel?"

"It's too hideous to have been in anyone's house," Jessica pointed out.

"We figure that the rugs were made inexpensively from carpet remnants, so we thought that it seems likely that they are being used in one of the dive hotels on the interstate," Jim commented. "Not that I would ever stay in one of those places, but Holiday Bay welcomes many visitors throughout the year. We figured someone might have mentioned the rugs."

"No," I answered. "I'm sorry. I don't think I've ever heard anyone commenting about a rug quite like that."

"Too bad," Jim said. "A pink and blue rug sounds like a decent clue if you ask me."

I found that I had to agree with that. I doubted there were many rugs quite like that to be found in our community, or any community, for that matter.

Chapter 7

"Cam and I are meeting the complex manager and doing a walkthrough at the condo at nine-thirty," Amy informed me the following morning. "As long as everything is good, we should get the keys once we've completed the walkthrough."

"Congratulations. I'm really excited for you. Do you need someone to cover the lunch shift in the kitchen?"

"No. I'm heading in now to do the prep, and we should be back before the Bistro opens. If, for some reason, we aren't done with the walkthrough by eleven, I'll just let Cam finish up at the condo and head back to the Bistro, so don't worry about not having a chef onsite by the time we open. We originally asked to do the walkthrough tomorrow or even Monday, but the complex manager is heading out of town for a few days and wanted to get it done before he left. We've already seen the place, so it shouldn't take long."

"Okay. Thanks for letting me know. I imagine getting the keys today will allow you to begin moving in tomorrow."

"That's the plan." She poured coffee into a travel mug. "Where's Dawson?"

"He got up early and is in the garage tuning the Harley. We talked about heading out for a nice long ride tomorrow, and he wanted to check things over since he hasn't ridden it since last fall."

"Tomorrow should be a nice day for a ride, and I think the weather is supposed to be just about perfect, but I did hope we could use his muscles and truck to move a few larger items over to the condo."

"I guess you can ask him. If I know Dawson, which I do, he won't mind helping you. We can take a ride on Monday. In fact, it seems that the weather is supposed to be even better on Monday."

"That's how the weather woman on Channel Two made it sound. Sunny skies, low humidity, nice and warm, but not too hot. We seem to have experienced about as nice of a spring as we've had in the past few years."

"I agree. It has been nice."

After Amy headed into the garage to ask Dawson about helping with the move, I headed back upstairs to shower and dress for the day. Dawson's shift in the bar didn't start until two again today, but the Bistro opened at eleven-thirty, so I planned to be there by ten-thirty. I expected it to be a busy day with the nice weather, and given that we didn't currently have a dining room manager, I figured it was a good idea for me to be there early to ensure everyone showed up on time and that there weren't any issues that needed to be addressed. Not that the staff not showing up on time was a problem. I had an excellent team, but since Rosalyn had quit, I felt it was more important to be there myself. If I wanted to return to a comfortable pace with my hours, I supposed I would need to hire someone to take Rosalyn's place. On a whim, I decided to call Harlee. When I explained who I was and why I was calling, she sounded surprised to hear that her grandfather had spoken to Nikki about her, but she also agreed to meet me at the Bistro at ten-thirty.

"Are you heading out?" Dawson asked me after I poked my head into the garage to let him know I was doing just that.

"I decided to go ahead and interview the woman I told you about yesterday. She sounded surprised when I called, so I don't think her grandfather necessarily planned to pass her name along to me. Or at least he hadn't mentioned it to her beforehand, but I figured we need a dining room manager, and it never hurts to talk to potential applicants."

Dawson wiped his hands on a rag and then tossed the rag on the workbench. "I don't disagree, but I also think we should take our time and make sure we find someone who isn't only qualified but fits in the family we already have in place."

"I totally agree, and I just plan to speak with the woman. I'd never hire anyone without talking to you and Amy first. Speaking of Amy, did she ask you about helping her and Cam with their move?"

"She did. Since it looks like the bike needs a part, we'll need to postpone our cruise in the countryside, so I told Amy I'd help her. She seems excited about settling in her new place, and I guess I don't blame her."

"Amy's worked hard to get to a point in her life where she can afford such a nice place, and I'm really happy for her."

"It will certainly be nice to have the house all to ourselves for a few months. Not that I don't love Amy, and you know I adore your sisters, but time with just you, me, Goliath, and the cats sounds pretty special."

"It will be nice," I agreed. I glanced at my watch. "I really need to run if I'm not going to be late meeting Harlee. Any idea what time you'll be in?"

"I'm going to head in and clean up now. Leo called and wants to chat with me about the situation with Cayson. I told him I'd stop by his place on my way into town, but I shouldn't be too long."

"Situation with Cayson? Are you referring to the fact that he seems to be a suspect in the murder of Gavin Houghton?"

"I am. I guess you heard that there's a vocal group in town who have basically tried and convicted Cayson for Gavin's death. At least in their minds, since he hasn't even been charged with anything. This group is sure he's guilty, and they're putting pressure on Colt to formally arrest the guy. So far, all Colt has done is chat with him, but this does seem to be developing into one of those situations where the burden of proof seems to be on Cayson."

"So rather than being innocent until proven guilty, it's a case of being guilty until proven innocent."

"Basically. Alex is in a tough spot since she wants to help Cayson, but she has a job to do. If someone even thinks that she shows too much favoritism for the guy, it won't help his case. There are already those saying she should be sidelined and not allowed to be involved with the investigation."

"So Leo is hoping that you can help him."

"He wants me to look into some things. He didn't say what he wanted me to look into... just that we needed to talk. I told him I'd stop by, and that's where we left it. I'll catch you up once I have more information."

"I'd appreciate that. And I hope you can help Alex, Leo, and Cayson. At this point, I don't have an opinion about Cayson's guilt or innocence, but Alex and Leo are good people. They don't deserve the backlash certain groups in town are sending in their direction."

I headed toward the house with Dawson after he locked up the garage. He scrubbed his hands with a degreasing solution while I leaned against the laundry room counter near the sink.

"I feel bad for Alex," I said as I thought things over. "She really is in a tough position."

"She really is. I also think Leo is trying to keep her out of his independent investigation to whatever degree he can. Colt is a fair guy, and I certainly don't see him caving into pressure from the particular group of locals who are sure that Cayson is to blame for the death of the town manager. Although, I also suspect he's experienced enough to know that he will need to tread lightly if he doesn't want to create a much larger problem."

I glanced at the clock. "I really do need to go. I realize I said that before, but I intend to do so this time. Let's talk later."

I handed Dawson a towel to dry his hands. He kissed me, and I headed toward the driveway where I'd left my car. As I passed Cayson's house on my way into town, I noticed that someone had spray painted the words 'once a killer, always a killer' on the side of his garage. I wasn't sure if Cayson was guilty of killing the liquor store clerk in Baltimore he'd been convicted of killing or if he'd been innocent of that man's death as he claimed, but I was pretty sure that despite the conflict between them, it hadn't been Cayson who'd killed Houghton. If the burden of proof was on Cayson, I planned to help him to the highest degree possible.

When I arrived at the Bistro, I found that Amy and Cambria were both there. I hoped everything had gone smoothly and there hadn't been a hitch since things seemed to have gone much more quickly than expected.

"You're back already?" I asked after joining them in the kitchen.

"The complex manager was in a rush, so we just walked through, made a few notes on the walkthrough form, signed it, got the keys, and left," Amy informed me. "The place was in pretty good shape, so there wasn't much to note. The complex manager said if we found anything during the move-in that wasn't noted, we could take a photo of the issue and text it to him, and he would add it to the form."

It sounded as if the complex manager was pretty easygoing, which would likely make things easier on the new roommates. "I have an interview with Harlee, the potential dining room manager Nikki told us about. She'll be in shortly, so I should head back downstairs, but we should chat after."

"Is this the woman whose grandfather requested the interview?" Cambria asked.

I confirmed that it was, and I added that the woman seemed surprised when I'd called, so I wasn't even sure that Harlee was looking for a job, but I figured it would be beneficial to at least have a conversation with her.

When I entered the dining room, Harlee was chatting with Nikki at the hostess stand. I introduced myself and then showed her to a table in the corner.

"I appreciate you taking the time to meet with me," Harlee said after we were seated. "My grandfather is such a sweetheart, and I know he asked that you speak with me because he wants nothing more than the best for me. But the reality is that my reason for moving from Florida to Maine in the first place was to help my grandparents so they could remain in their home for a while longer." She folded her hands on the table in front of her. "I'd like to be working again. Having a job might help me make friends, and friends would allow me to have my own life outside of the life I share with my grandparents. But the reality is that my grandparents need quite a lot of help. Something part-time might work out okay, but a job as a dining room manager sounds like more than I'd be able to handle."

"I understand. In fact, I actually had a similar thought when I first heard your grandfather's request. Do your grandparents need around-the-clock care?"

"No, they can do many things for themselves, but they are limited. They have a car, but they really shouldn't drive. Neither have the range of motion or the eyesight it takes to be a safe driver, although neither will admit that. I haven't gotten anywhere by trying to get them to take the senior bus, a rideshare, or public transportation, so I make sure to be there to help with transportation for doctors' appointments, shopping, and other errands. In terms of tasks around the house, they can handle simple chores like making their own bed, but they need help with heavy cleaning, snow removal, and even yard work. They have a guy who comes around to mow during lawn season, but there's more involved with tending the yard than just mowing."

"I suppose you could hire a full-time gardener."

"We could, but there are other reasons for me to be there as often as possible." She paused, likely to gather her thoughts, and then continued. "Just a few days ago, my grandmother made a big batch of her famous spaghetti. She'd initially filled a pot for the pasta by placing it on the stove and then using a smaller pitcher to fill it with water. That was actually a good way to fill the pot. The problem was that once the water boiled and she'd cooked the pasta, she didn't have a way to drain the water. When I entered the kitchen, she was trying to lift the heavy pot without any help. She would never have made it to the sink without dropping it. I could tell she was frustrated by her lack of strength, but it would have been much worse to spill boiling water down the front of herself."

"It sounds as if a part-time position would fit with your other responsibilities much better than a full-time job. Unfortunately, I don't have any part-time openings to offer you, but we will need help for the summer if you're interested."

"Can I think about it? On the one hand, since I live with my grandparents rent-free, I don't need a lot of money, but it would be nice to be able to pay my own way and not have to ask them for money to have a meal out or buy personal items at a store. On the other hand, as I've already pointed out, my schedule would need to be flexible since I would still need to be able to drive my grandparents to doctors' appointments and that sort of thing. Maybe working on Saturdays and Sundays since they tend to stay in on weekends."

"It might be possible to make that work once the summer rush kicks in. Have you done anything other than work in food service?"

She nodded. "Actually, I have. Before I moved from Florida, I was working to build my own bookkeeping business. I worked at the restaurant because I had rent and other bills to worry about, but while working there, I was also working on obtaining all my certifications and then finding clients for my service."

"Bookkeeping?" I asked, immediately interested in exploring the idea. "Do you have references from your clients in Florida?"

"I do. Do you know someone who needs a bookkeeper?"

"I actually might have a bookkeeping position open for the right person. The books would need to be kept current, as would the inventory, and tasks such as payroll would need to be done on a predetermined day of the week, but in general, the job would be flexible. In fact, much of the work could be done remotely from your home." I supposed that hiring someone I'd just met to do my books was a risk, but I figured that anyone who would give up her life to help her grandparents must be trustworthy. "If you think you might be open to the idea, I'll need to check your references, and then I'll want to talk about it with my two co-owners, but if you're interested, I'd like to keep the discussion going."

"I'm very interested," Harlee said. "I can either print my resume and drop it back by in a few hours or email it to you."

"Email is fine."

"The resume includes a work history, a list of prior clients, schooling and certifications, and references."

"That should work just fine."

She pulled her cell phone out. "I have the resume in the cloud, so if you give me the email you'd like it sent to, I can send it to you before I leave."

I rattled off my business email address. Then, I thanked the young woman for coming in and told her I looked forward to speaking to her again once I had the time to follow up on a few things.

After Harlee left, I headed to the kitchen to speak with Amy about the idea. Dawson hadn't come in yet, but since Amy knew I was meeting with Harlee, I predicted she'd be interested in the outcome of our conversation.

"If this woman really does have a background in bookkeeping, it sounds like an opportunity that might be too good not to at least follow up on," Amy said. "I know how much you hate doing the bookkeeping."

"I really do hate it. When we initially bought the Bistro, and I decided to handle the books myself rather than hiring a firm to take care of the paperwork, I had no idea how time-consuming that part of my job would be. I have ideas for special events that I believe would help grow our customer base I just haven't had time to implement. Having more time to commit to the aspects of my job that I believe I would genuinely enjoy doing would be nice."

"It sounds to me that it might be time to hire someone to do the books, whether Harlee works out or not," Cambria said.

I supposed I agreed with that.

"I spoke to Dawson about helping us move tomorrow," Amy said. "He said he needed to order a part for the motorcycle, so he was happy to help us. I hope that's okay with you. I suppose Cam and I are somewhat intruding on your 'couple time.'"

"It's more than fine," I assured her. "And I'm happy to help as well. We'll likely bring Goliath. Are the condos pet friendly?"

"They are," Amy assured me. "Honestly, I've been trying to decide if I should bring Marley with me or leave him at your place where he has Hennessy for company when no one is home. Assuming it's okay with you, at least for now, I think I'll leave him where he is."

"That's fine with me. Goliath loves Marley."

"Speaking of Goliath, where is he?"

"Dawson will bring him in. He needed to stop and chat with Leo on his way to work, so he'll be in later."

"Speaking of Leo, I heard that Lucas Manfield and some of his buddies are mad that Dawson is helping Leo with Cayson's defense," Cambria said.

"He's not actually helping Leo with Cayson's defense since Cayson hasn't actually been arrested and doesn't actually need a defense, but I guess he is helping Leo to prove that Cayson didn't kill Houghton, which now that I say that out loud, I realize is pretty much the same thing."

"I think it's nice of Leo to try to help Cayson, and I think it's nice of Dawson to want to help Leo, but there are some pretty damming arguments out there as to why Cayson really should be behind bars while Colt and his team try to figure this all out," Cam added.

"Damming arguments?" I asked.

Cam stopped what she was doing and gave me her full attention. "I guess you heard that Houghton's body was found wrapped in a rug."

"I did hear that," I said.

"Did you hear that before the rug was wrapped around Houghton's body, it was on the floor in Cayson's living room?"

I raised a brow. "It was?" I guess I'd never been inside the Boston home, so there was no way I could have known that.

"In all fairness, the rug had been on the floor in the Boston home when Elsa Boston was alive, and once Cayson began to remodel the place, he removed the rug from the house and stored it in the shed," Amy added.

"So if the rug was being stored in the shed, then anyone who knew it was there could have stolen it and used it to frame Cayson," I said.

While Cambria agreed that was possible, she also pointed out that for that to have happened, the person who was trying to frame Cayson would not only have to have known about the rug and where it was stored, but they would also have to have the opportunity to steal it without Cayson knowing it was even gone.

"Someone spray-painted his garage," I said. "At this point, no one knows who did it. At a minimum, I guess it is possible to sneak onto the Boston property, commit an act of vandalism, and get away before anyone knows you were there."

Cam admitted that I made a good point. Of course, she also argued that Cayson and our murder victim had been arguing just hours before the man was murdered and that Cayson had made some pretty firm comments about shutting the man up. If Cayson was innocent, as I hoped he was, then the only way naysayers like Lucas Manfield and the other locals he'd riled up were ever going to be satisfied that Caleb really wasn't their man was to prove beyond a shadow of a doubt that someone else did it.

Chapter 8

"Hey, Shelby, you have a call on the landline," Lucy said the moment I set foot on the first floor of the Bistro after speaking to Amy and Cambria.

"Do you know who it is?"

"Someone from the high school, I think."

I suppressed a groan. It was Saturday. Why on earth would Charise be calling me on a Saturday? I supposed it might be someone else, but offhand, I couldn't think of who, other than Charise, would be calling from the high school.

"I'll take the call in my office," I said. "Which line?"

"Two."

I took a deep breath before picking the phone up. *Patience, Shelby. This woman knows a lot of people. You need to be nice to her*, I said to myself. Blowing out the breath I'd just taken, I greeted the woman. "Charise. I'm so sorry to keep you waiting. How can I help you?"

"I had breakfast with some of the others on the luncheon committee, and they had a few tiny suggestions."

"Okay," I said, picking up a pen and notepad. "What sort of suggestions are we looking at?"

Luckily, since the items on Charise's list of changes to the décor and the menu were minimal, they actually wouldn't be a problem at this point. I once again reminded the woman that I would need to finalize things as we approached the event, and she assured me that these would be the last changes she'd need to make.

"I guess you've heard all the hoopla about Gavin Houghton's murder," Charise tacked onto the end of our conversation. I thought the fact that she brought up the subject was odd since I hadn't mentioned it, but I decided to see where she was going with this.

"Yes. I have heard about the murder. It's always such a tragedy when a member of the community dies in such a violent manner."

"I'm not sure that I'd call what happened to Houghton a tragedy, but I suppose how things played out was unfortunate. I understand that the nice young man, Cayson, who is building the dog rescue facility, has been targeted as a suspect."

"I don't have the specifics, but I understand he was brought in for questioning. Do you know Cayson?"

"I don't know him well, but I got my car stuck in a snowbank after sliding off the road this past winter, and Cayson just happened to be driving by. He stopped, and after he dug me out, he followed me all the way home to ensure that I arrived safely since, according to him, my tires weren't adequate for the current road conditions."

"That was nice of him," I agreed.

"It definitely was, which is why I feel so bad that the guy might have given into his impulse and killed another man."

"I don't think there is any proof that Cayson killed anyone. I guess he was called in for questioning, but I think part of the reason for that is because he was seen arguing with Houghton shortly before he died."

"Yes, well, you can blame Houghton for any argument that may have occurred. The man wasn't the best type of person, if you know what I mean."

Since I was unsure of the meaning behind her statement but wanted to understand it, I asked her to provide some clarification.

"Gavin Houghton had a decent reputation here in Holiday Bay. Not perfect, but decent enough that folks tended to go along with whatever he wanted to do. The thing that not everyone understood, however, was that the man was ambitious. Very ambitious. If he needed to use someone or step over them to get what he wanted, then that was what he would do. The man was very focused and didn't think the rules applied to him. That made him dangerous."

"So, did he act outside the law at times?"

"He did, but of course, you didn't hear that from me."

I frowned. "So, who do you think killed Houghton?"

She paused and then answered. "I can't say for sure, but if I were you and I was interested in the answer to that question, I'd have a discussion with River Overland."

"River Overland?" I asked. River was a local conservationist who worked tirelessly to preserve the area's history. He and his group from the historical society had successfully stopped several development projects from being built on historical and sensitive land.

"Houghton was helping Jethro Paul obtain permits to tear down the old seaport building. River and his group were blocking them at every turn, but it seemed as if, with Houghton's help, the developer was making progress. As far as I know, the whole thing is still tied up in court, but things had been moving along nicely until Houghton died. There was a point where I thought River might throw in the towel and admit defeat, but with Houghton out of the way, suddenly, saving the old building seems possible."

I guessed I could see where Charise was coming from, but River seemed to be a peaceful man who wouldn't harm a fly. Still, I believed it was worth sharing this tip with someone, although I needed to process this before I got into things too intensely with Charise. Still, I was interested in knowing how she knew what she knew, so I asked.

"My husband is an attorney who plays golf with the town's attorney. They talk. Sometimes, they talk while having an after-game drink on my patio, and I listen in."

"So, do you know anything specific about the situation or who else might have been involved?" I asked.

"Not really. I only listen. I don't ask questions. And if you are thinking of sharing this news with anyone, remember, no one can know that any of this came from me. What I overheard was likely attorney-client privilege, and even if it wasn't, my husband would kill me if he knew that I'd repeated even a single word of anything I'd overheard during one of his rants with other attorneys he socializes with. You can't tell anyone I told you what I have. If you do, I'll deny it. Honestly, I'm not even sure why I've said what I have, but I guess that knowing what I know has been heavy on my mind, and now that a man is dead, my need to pass the information along has been almost overwhelming."

I wanted Charise to tell Colt, or perhaps Alex, what she told me, but if she couldn't or wouldn't, I supposed I would.

Chapter 9

"So, do you think that River Overland had something to do with Gavin Houghton's murder?" Alex asked me later that evening. It was after six o'clock, and she just happened to have stopped in for a bite to eat since Leo was meeting with Cayson and the construction crew, and she was at loose ends until he was freed up around eight.

"It's a theory," I said. "It's not a theory I necessarily agree with since I've never known River to be anything other than a passivist, but it is a theory that has been floated to me."

"I've heard the scuttlebutt about the old seaport building. Did you know that the building was built more than a century ago? It truly should be preserved rather than torn down, but I guess change is inevitable, so there are times when those with a foot in the past need to take a step into the future. Having said that, I really don't think that River would bludgeon Gavin to death, and even if he was the one to have killed the man, he certainly wouldn't try to frame Cayson. Cayson and River have actually become friends. Cayson even plans to donate time to help the historical society with a couple renovations they've been trying to set aside funding for."

"If it is true that the killer is trying to frame Cayson, then I guess we need to find someone who wanted both men out of the way. Are you sure that the killer didn't merely use Cayson's rug because it was discarded and wouldn't be missed, and not as a means of intentionally framing the guy?" I asked.

"Not likely. I hate to say this, but unless we can come up with a suspect other than Cayson, he will likely become the sacrificial lamb."

"Maybe we can have Dawson do a deep dive into Houghton," I suggested. "I realize that he's the victim and not the killer, but if we can figure out a motive for someone other than Cayson or River and his group to want him dead, that may lead to the killer."

"I'm game, but I'll need to tread lightly and be careful about what I say and how involved I am. I don't want to do anything that might hurt Cayson and the delicate line he needs to walk."

"Do you have any suspects in Houghton's murder? Anyone other than Cayson, that is?"

"No," Alex answered. She paused thoughtfully. "I guess that's not entirely true, but, at this point, there isn't anyone I can talk about."

"Understood. Let's go and talk to Dawson."

Even when Dawson was busy, he was always happy to help, so he turned things over to Nikki and followed Alex and me to a booth in the corner. "I'm happy to do some digging," Dawson said after Alex brought him up to speed on the investigation. "As long as you don't arrest me."

"I won't, but I can't speak for other members of law enforcement. Not Colt or even Brax. They wouldn't. But the sheriff and state police are both involved." Alex referred to the newest officer assigned to assist Police Chief Colt Wilder, Braxton Baker.

"Noted," Dawson said. "I'll tread lightly, but it does appear that Cayson is being intentionally set up. The fact that the body was wrapped in a rug that was being stored in Cayson's shed is so obvious. In fact, in my mind, this seems to prove his innocence. The guy has been to prison. He's street-smart. If he did kill Houghton, there's no way he'd wrap him in a rug that would point directly to him."

"I agree," Alex said. "The problem is that a group of individuals in the community simply want Cayson gone. They don't seem to care if he's innocent or guilty of killing Houghton or even if he's innocent or guilty of the shooting in Baltimore. These individuals have merely concluded that Cayson is a bad seed and want him removed from their community."

"That is just so unfair," I said.

Alex and Dawson agreed.

"Alex was right when she said that we're going to need to come up with an alternate suspect," Dawson said. "A good one. One who will draw the focus away from Cayson. I can start with the basics. Phone and financial records and that sort of thing, but we'll need more. At this point, I feel like we're going to need a smoking gun."

"I can forward you the police file," Alex said. "It's pretty thin at this point. All we know is where the body was found and that the cause of death was blunt force trauma to the head. It appears he was struck repeatedly with an object, likely a bat, but there may be other options. We've spoken to friends, neighbors, and coworkers who brought up the fact that Houghton has been on a campaign to run Cayson out of town, but they also all said they weren't aware of any other conflicts he might have been engaged in that would have led to his death. Colt, Brax, and I all plan to put our full effort into this, but we truly could use a break."

Alex's cell phone beeped. She looked at the caller ID and frowned. "It's Colt. I need to call him back. I'm going to head out to the parking lot. I shouldn't be long."

After Alex left to make her call, I asked Dawson about his conversation with Leo. Leo had asked Dawson to look into three individuals a man who didn't want to be identified had targeted as possible suspects in Houghton's death, but he hadn't gotten around to it yet. I asked who he was looking at, and Dawson admitted that he didn't recognize the names but had written them down. The list was in his jacket pocket, and the jacket was in my office. I offered to run upstairs and get the list. Maybe Alex could tell us more about the three men on the list. As I reached for the list in Dawson's jacket pocket, I saw an envelope on my desk bearing my name. I hadn't noticed it before, so I assumed someone left it for me since I'd last worked at my desk earlier in the day. I picked up the envelope, opened it, and read the note.

If you don't want your business to be burned, let the convict burn.

Let the convict burn? Whoever left the note must be referring to Cayson. I had to assume that the person who sent the note didn't mean I should literally allow Cayson to burn. At least, I hoped not. I grabbed the envelope, note, and Dawson's list and headed downstairs. I handed the list to Dawson and then showed him the note.

"Any idea where this came from?" he asked.

"No clue. I'm going to check with the dining room staff."

In addition to Dawson, I only had nine staff members on shift today. Since I doubted that Amy or Cambria had been downstairs to receive the envelope, I started by speaking with Charmaine, who was managing the dining room today.

"Hey, Charmaine, I'm trying to figure out who put this envelope on my desk. Was it you?"

"No. When was it left?"

"I'm not sure. It could have been at any point this afternoon."

"I guess you can check with Lucy or Nikki. Lucy ran upstairs to ask for a quick side she forgot to order, and Nikki is covering the bar now, but she was in the dining room earlier. Jody was likewise downstairs earlier, but I sent her to the rooftop to help Harrington and Clifton with the dinner rush."

"And Pru?"

"She had to get to her other job, so I let her go. The rooftop is packed, but things are slow downstairs. I don't have a shift at the Roundup tonight, so I can stay as long as you need me."

"Thanks, Charmaine. I appreciate you staying late. I would have offered you more hours today, but I figured you had a shift at the Roundup. You usually work there on the weekends."

"I do, but I'm having a few issues with the new bartender. I honestly might quit. I probably would have quit by now, but I make good tips at the Roundup. A lot better than I could ever make here."

"The dining room manager position is still open if you want to reconsider that. I realize that you said that you couldn't commit to those sorts of hours due to your job at the Roundup when I asked before, but if things have gotten difficult there, I'd still love to talk to you about it."

She paused. "Maybe. Are you sure Nikki doesn't want it?"

"I've asked her about it three times, and she said no each time. At this point, I think she wants to focus on building a life with Nick. She's commented that she doesn't want to get tied down to a job with lots of responsibility. I believe we both know that she could do it if she wanted to since, like you, she's been around long enough to know what to do and when to do it. But she's still in her twenties, and I don't think she's ready for the level of responsibility a management job would require."

"Okay," Charmaine said. "Let me think about it. I'd hate to say I'd take it, only to change my mind if the new bartender at the Roundup ends up getting canned. We both know I tend to run hot and cold with most jobs I take on, at least to this point. But I promise that I will really think it through. If I don't feel capable of fully committing to all the responsibilities of being your dining room manager, I'll continue doing my current duties. If I do, however, decide to commit, you can count on me to be all in."

I reached out and gave her a hug. "Thanks. That's all I can ask for."

A group came in looking to be seated, which demanded Charmaine's attention, so I headed across the room to ask Lucy about the envelope. It took a few minutes, but eventually, I was able to determine that Jody was the one who put the envelope on my desk. Claw, one of the men who worked the lobster boats, had brought it in when he'd come in with his buddies. Claw asked Jody to give me the envelope, and since I'd been otherwise occupied, she put it on my desk. Claw was still at the bar, so I asked him if he was the one who wrote the note inside the envelope. He said that he hadn't written the note and that a tall man with sand-colored hair wearing a dark blue sleeveless t-shirt had handed him the envelope, along with a fifty-dollar bill, and asked him to deliver the envelope to me. He didn't know the man's name and, in fact, claimed that he'd never even seen him before, but fifty bucks would buy beer for the crew, so it seemed like a simple request when compared to the amount of cash being offered.

"So some guy gives one of the lobstermen fifty bucks to deliver to you this message," Alex confirmed. "Why? Fifty bucks seems like a lot. Why not mail it to you or merely drop it off himself?"

"No idea," I responded. "I guess whoever delivered it didn't want to be recognized."

"Tall with sand-colored hair is a pretty general description," Beck commented after I told him about the note I found on my desk. "I doubt asking around will do us a lot of good. Unless, of course, Claw can remember something unique like a scar, tattoo, or other unique identifier." Beck glanced at the bar. "Claw is still here. I'll go and talk to him."

I turned my attention to Alex. "Is everything okay? I know you stepped outside to speak with Colt earlier."

"Colt wanted to let me know that a new piece of evidence has been brought forward, and the DA is pushing for an arrest in the Gavin Houghton murder case."

"Cayson?"

She nodded.

"What sort of evidence are we talking about?"

"A bat with Cayson's name on it was found in the dumpster at the construction site by one of the other men. The bat had blood on it."

"So does the DA think the bat with Cayson's name on it was used to kill Houghton?" I asked.

She nodded once again.

"I have so many questions at this point."

"I can only imagine. I had a lot of questions as well when Colt shared the news. Questions like why does a bat with Cayson's name on it even exist? And, by the way, the answer to that question is that the bat had been Cayson's when he was a kid playing in Little League, and his mom had written his name on it so it wouldn't get mixed up with bats owned by other team members."

I supposed that made sense.

Alex continued. "Colt asked Cayson if he'd discarded his bat in the dumpster at the construction site for some reason, and Cayson said he hadn't seen that old bat since he was a kid, and he didn't even know his mother still had it. He suspected it had been in the shed with all the other items she had stored there."

"Is Colt going to arrest the guy?" I asked.

"Not yet. While we have some circumstantial evidence to support such a move, nothing is concrete. As for the blood on the bat, at this point, we don't even know whether it's human blood or not. And even if it is human blood, we don't know if it will be a match for Houghton's blood. And even if that turns out to be the case, we have no proof that Cayson was the person who used the bat."

"If Cayson is the killer, it seems highly unlikely to me that he'd just toss the murder weapon in the dumpster at the construction site where anyone could find it," I said.

"Exactly," Alex agreed. "In my mind, and in Colt's, the fact that the bat was tossed in the dumpster at the construction site seems to add legitimacy to the idea that Cayson is being set up." She took a breath and then continued. "Of course, the mayor is just looking for us to make an arrest, and the DA seems to be all over the idea that Cayson is the guilty party. Colt told me that he told the DA that he was working on nailing down something solid, but between you and me, I don't think he has anything solid. At this point, he's just trying to buy time while we dig something up. Colt and I plan to meet at the station in the morning and discuss things." Alex looked at her cell phone. "I need to start wrapping this up. Leo has Coop and Fisher with him, and we talked about just meeting at the beach to walk the dogs when he was finished. He said he should be done at eight. Since it's seven-forty now, I'll text him to confirm, but before I go, who are the three men on the list."

Dawson read the note. "Stanton Cook, Forsyth Press, and Austin Jasper."

"And who gave Leo the list?" Alex asked.

"He didn't say. I guess you can try asking him. Leo didn't recognize any of the names on the list either, but he didn't want to discount the tip as being bogus without actually looking into it."

"I'll ask him about it when I get home," Alex said. "In the meantime, let's stay in touch."

Dawson needed to return to the bar since the after-dinner crowd had begun to arrive, but I didn't have anything pressing to take care of, so I figured I'd hang out in the bar with Dawson until it was time to close for the night. The Bistro was closed on Sundays and Mondays, which meant Dawson and I had two days off. We'd committed to helping Amy and Cambria move tomorrow, but perhaps we could take Goliath and do something fun the following day.

Chapter 10

Amy was up before the sun, which I supposed I understood. There was one thing that could be said for new beginnings. Most of the time, although definitely not every time, new beginnings were an opportunity to open the door to a life even better than the one you'd had before. I was going to miss Amy, but I could see that she was excited about the idea of being out on her own. I supposed that the temporary living arrangement we made when we'd first opened the Bistro had extended far beyond what either of us had anticipated it would.

"Are you all packed?" I asked Amy after I went down to the kitchen for coffee.

"I am. I'm loading my car now with as many boxes as I can. I'll drop everything off at the condo, and then Cam and I will come here to start loading the larger pieces we hoped to have Dawson's help with."

"Dawson is in the shower, but we're committed to helping you and Cambria today. We'll take as many loads as you need us to take."

She crossed the room and hugged me. "Thanks, Shelby." She looked around. "I've been really excited about the condo and didn't think I'd be feeling teary-eyed to move out of my room here, but apparently, I was wrong about that. I know I'll still see you at work practically every day, but somehow, it just won't be the same."

"I know what you mean," I replied, fighting back my tears. "In a way, I guess things have already changed. Now that Dawson has moved in with me, you and I no longer have our late-night gab sessions. I do miss that. Don't get me wrong, I'm thrilled to have Dawson in my life, but what he and I have is different from what you and I had. I'm really going to miss that."

"You can come over and spend the night with Cam and me whenever you want to. On those occasions when I stayed at Cam's apartment, we started the custom of slipping into our flannel pajamas, curling up with a cup of hot cocoa close to a roaring fire, and talking about our day the way you and I did in the beginning."

It was true that unwinding with a friend was much different than unwinding with a love interest.

"I'm going to run upstairs and get dressed so that I'm ready to help when you're ready for me."

"Cam and I should be here to load the big items in about two hours," she said. "I'll bring breakfast sandwiches."

"And I'll make a fresh pot of coffee," I offered.

Dawson was coming out of the bathroom just as I was getting ready to go in. He asked about a timeline, and I shared my conversation with Amy. He responded that two hours would be perfect since there were a few things that he wanted to do on his computer before we started moving furniture. He headed into our home office, and I headed into the shower.

When Dawson came downstairs and joined me, it was almost time for Amy and Cambria to arrive.

"Did you get your work done?" I asked as Dawson poured a cup of coffee.

"I did. I've had a theory I wanted to test and decided to open a CHOMP account so that I would see exactly how it works. Charmaine knows a guy who's a member, and he was willing to refer me so I could get a link to access the site. The buy-in amount was substantial, which I anticipated, but it was much more substantial than expected."

"How much?" I asked.

"Ten grand."

I whistled. "That is a lot. I'm surprised that so many people are willing to do that."

"Based on the information I was able to dig up, the payout is significant, and the odds of winning are infinitely better than other forms of online betting."

"That still seems like a lot."

"I agree, but the odds of winning something is only about one in ten. Of course, the odds of winning the multimillion-dollar pot are pretty astronomical."

"So there are smaller pots to win?" I asked.

"There are. Quite a few, actually. And I think this is part of the secret of CHOMP's success. The psychology of gambling is interesting. While logic would dictate otherwise, it is often the case that someone who places bets for a thousand dollars and then wins one of the lesser pots, even though that pot may only be worth five hundred dollars, that person will come away from that experience feeling like a winner."

That was crazy in my book, but I guessed I could see how winning any of the pots would still provide the satisfaction of having won. "So, did you actually buy in for ten grand?"

"I did," Dawson answered. "I only plan to poke around a bit, maybe participate in a low-dollar game or two, and then cash out my entire account, but I figured that by buying in, I will have access to the site. Today is Sunday. The email with next week's games will arrive on Tuesday. That gives me a couple of days to poke around and try to determine if there is anything more sinister going on than illegal gambling."

"Do you think something more is going on?"

"Not necessarily. The fact that Caleb was involved in the game before the accident does provide a link of sorts to the man, but not a strong link to his death."

"Do you think there's any chance at all that Caleb is still alive? It seems to look that way, but we still don't know if that's true with any degree of certainty."

Dawson rolled his lips. "I'm not sure, although the evidence does seem to be stacking up to support the idea that he might have faked his death."

Amy and Cambria showed up with breakfast sandwiches at this point, causing us to end our conversation, eat, and then focus on the move. The condo the women leased really was gorgeous. The flooring was a light gray wood grain porcelain that, while looking like real wood, possessed the ease of maintenance that could be found only with tile. The walls were painted a soft sky blue and were accented by white baseboards and ceiling trim. The granite in the kitchen was a deep blue, and the appliances, which looked new, were black stainless, which was actually more of a gray color. Of course, the biggest draw to the upgraded space was the huge windows that looked out over a gentle sea rolling onto a sandy beach.

"This view really is breathtaking," I said. I opened one of the sliding glass doors and stepped outside. The patio was small but was strategically situated so that sitting on one of the padded chairs would provide a perfect view of the sunrise. "I can imagine you having coffee out here during the summer when the mornings are mild."

"That's the plan," Amy said. "And we have both a fire pit and a patio heater for those mornings and evenings where it's dry enough to sit out but not quite warm enough."

The sound of the waves, accompanied by the squawking of birds on the beach, was almost hypnotic.

"We ordered new living room furniture, which hasn't been delivered yet, but come look at my bedroom," Amy said.

I followed Amy to the bedroom suite on the right side of the living space. Cambria had claimed the living space on the left side of the common area as her own.

"You have your own slider that provides exterior access without going through the living room," I said.

Amy nodded. "Both bedroom suites have a full bath, a small seating area, which I plan to use for a desk, and a glass slider that leads out onto a small patio area. Like I said, these units are pricy, but they're so perfect for Cam and me that we decided to make whatever cuts were needed to allow us to afford it."

Dawson began unloading the furniture we'd brought from Amy's room. It appeared that we'd only need one or maybe two more loads, which was a lot less than we'd anticipated, so when Goliath acted like he needed to take a potty break, we decided to walk him along the pretty little beach across the street before heading back into town for the second load.

"This really is a nice beach," I said as Dawson and I walked hand in hand, and Goliath trotted in front of us. "It's so flat and wide compared to many of the beaches in the area. And while I imagine that there are cars parked along the street during the summer, it's all but deserted today."

"It is nice," Dawson agreed. "I like that you can walk all the way to the dunes before you come to any obstacles."

"I think this is the same street where Gavin Houghton's body was found."

"It is," Dawson confirmed. "But the body was found about a half mile east of here."

"Do you know if Colt ever figured out where the man actually died? I seem to remember that it had been determined that he hadn't died where the body was found."

"As of the last time I asked anyone about it, they still hadn't determined where Houghton had died. Of course, that was a couple days ago, so that may have changed. If I would have thought about it, I would have asked Alex yesterday when we met to discuss the case."

"I guess we can call her later."

Dawson called for Goliath to slow down a bit since the gap between us had widened. "Actually," he answered. "I need to discuss the search I did relating to the three names on the list Leo gave me with both Alex and Leo. Maybe I'll call them and see if they can meet with us in a couple hours."

"That's fine with me. How about Beck? Should we ask him to join us?"

"Beck texted me earlier and said he had some things to discuss. He suggested that we get together with him and Lou for dinner."

"I wouldn't mind having dinner with Beck and Lou. Did he say where or when?"

"No, he just asked me to call him. I texted back and said I would once I got Amy's first load of furniture delivered."

"I suppose you can call him now," I suggested. "And then call Alex. Since it seems like we're about done here, maybe she can meet with us sooner rather than later."

As it turned out, Alex was in the area and said she'd come to us if we would wait for her since she had something to share. I glanced down the beach toward the old seaport where the building had stood proudly for over a century.

It only took a few minutes for Alex to arrive.

"That was fast," I said.

"I was at the old seaport building, which is close by. I ran into Joy this morning, and she told me about the year-round homeless population living in the building, so I went over to check things out since the scuttlebutt is that the building will be coming down soon."

Joy Christensen, an employee at Firehouse Books, had been penniless when she came to Holiday Bay with her family. As a result of her time trying to help her mother feed and house a family of five with no source of income, she'd befriended the men and women who lived in the transient camps in the area.

"Is the building definitely coming down?" I asked. "I heard that the whole thing was tied up in court."

"It is, but I spoke to Ariel, who told me that the developer seemed to be planning to take matters into his own hands, and I really needed to check it out. Ariel has always been a dependable source, so I decided to go and have a look for myself."

Ariel was a resident of a local homeless camp for five months out of the year by choice. She was educated and had a good job during the fall and winter, but come spring, she would set up a tent down on the beach and spend time with the "family" her grandfather had chosen as his own before he died.

"Did you find anything?" I asked.

"I found a homeless population living in the same space as an excessive amount of dynamite."

"Dynamite?" I asked. "That sounds like a less than ideal situation."

Alex looked back toward the building. "It could have been a catastrophic situation. I called Colt, and he, along with the bomb squad, are on the way. He had me evacuate everyone, and then he wanted me to get out of the building but to keep an eye on things, which I'm doing from here."

"Do you think it was the developer who killed Houghton?" Dawson asked. "I remember hearing that Houghton was working with the man, and it sounded like the developer might have gotten tired of all the red tape and decided to take things into his own hands."

Alex paused before answering. "I don't know. Maybe. While it's true that working through the legal channels was taking a long time, it seems like the developer may have decided that he was done waiting. Unfortunately, I've seen people do quite a few fairly awful things to their fellow man when money is involved." Alex looked toward the building she'd been watching. "Colt's here. I need to go." She looked at Dawson. "I likely won't be freed up to meet with you this afternoon as planned. Perhaps you should meet with Leo. He can catch me up."

"I'll do that," Dawson promised.

Dawson and I decided to call our dog so we could return to Amy and Cambria's condo and then head out for the second load. By this point, I was sure they were wondering where we were.

"We were about to call out search and rescue," Amy teased when we finally entered the condo through the front door.

"We would have been back much sooner, but we ran into Alex."

We then shared our story.

"Oh no. That's awful," Cambria said. "I can't believe someone was planning to blow that building up. And with people living there to boot. Did Alex know where the dynamite came from?"

"Not for sure, but she has her suspicions. At this point, I assume we can rest easy knowing that Alex and Colt are taking care of things." I looked at Amy. "Do we need to pick up anything else from our house, or should we head to Cam's apartment?"

"Let's head to Cam's. All I have left in my room are some boxes, and I can use my car to take them to the condo. Cam has a couple larger pieces of furniture, which we hope will fit in Dawson's truck."

Three additional trips were required to get everything, mainly because Cambria's dresser took up the entire bed of Dawson's truck and required a separate trip. Once we'd moved everything our friends needed to move, we needed to meet with Leo and then head home to get ready for our dinner with Beck and Lou.

Chapter 11

Dawson called Leo and arranged to meet him at his house once we finished helping Amy and Cambria. We figured we needed to go home anyway to clean up and change clothing before our dinner date with Beck and Lou, so meeting Leo at his home made the most sense since he lived right next door. When we arrived, we found Leo cleaning the temporary pens he'd put up to house the foster dogs he was taking care of until the construction of the rescue facility was completed.

"It looks like you have a full house," I said after walking over to one of the play areas filled with adorable puppies.

"It's puppy season. I'm fostering four mothers with pups right now. Fostering puppies is a lot of work, but at least once they're old enough, they're easier to place in forever homes than the adult dogs are." He held up his hands. "Just let me wash up, and we'll talk."

We followed Leo into the house. He offered us a cola, which we accepted, and then he suggested we sit out on the patio since it was such a nice day.

"So what did you find out?" Leo asked once we were settled.

"Before I go over my results, I really need to ask who gave you the list of names in the first place," Dawson said. "I know you said that the individual who gave you the list wanted to remain anonymous, but once I share the results of my research, I think you'll understand why I'm so interested."

Leo blew out a long breath and then answered. "It was Cory Stinson. On the one hand, I was suspicious from the beginning of our conversation since Cory is an electrician, and Cayson chose to go with another company for the current project. On the other hand, I've worked with Cory before, and he seems like a good guy. I've known him to be hardworking and honest. Not the sort who would go around spreading unsubstantiated rumors." Leo cleared his throat and then continued. "I did find it odd that Cory asked me not to share his identity with anyone. Cory indicated he was afraid about getting pulled into the whole mess and wanted to keep his distance, but he also felt he should share what he'd overheard. I took the list, but did think it odd that I didn't recognize a single name on it. I mean, how could these men be suspects in Houghton's murder if they weren't even locals."

"After looking into the men on the list you were given, I've come to the conclusion that Cory didn't give you the list as a means of identifying Houghton's killer or as a means of clearing Cayson's name, but as a means of solidifying any doubts you may have entertained about hiring Cayson in the first place."

Leo frowned. "What do you mean?"

"The men on the list aren't, as far as I can tell, in any way related to Houghton, the town, or the brutal murder of the town manager. I think Cory used the fact that Cayson was considered to be the main suspect in Houghton's murder as a reason to suggest that you investigate these men. If you'd investigated the men yourself rather than asking me to do it on your behalf, you would have found that all three men played a dominant role in Cayson's past."

"Role?"

Dawson nodded. "Stanton Cook actually goes by the nickname The Cook. He's a meth dealer who Cayson was in deep with during his time in Baltimore. Cayson was arrested twice for selling the meth Stanton cooked up, but I think it was the crimes committed by Cook and his men that Cory likely wanted you to be aware of. By linking Cayson and Cook, I think Cory hoped to cause you to see Cayson in a different light. A negative light. Cook is a hardcore criminal who has done despicable things. Being linked in any way to this man wouldn't be good for anyone's reputation."

Leo ran a hand through his hair. "I see. And the others?"

"Forsyth Press was killed in a hit-and-run accident while out jogging. He had a wife and three children. Lester Renfrew, the man who was eventually convicted of the death, insisted that Cayson was driving, not him. Cayson was adamant that he hadn't even been in the vehicle at the time of the accident and seemed to have proof to support that fact, so he wasn't charged. But, if you read the court transcripts, there is undeniably room for clarification in the timeline."

"Let me guess. Austin Jasper is the name of the man Cayson actually went to prison for killing."

Dawson nodded. "You've known from the beginning that he had a past. You've known Cayson had been in prison for a crime he insisted he was innocent of, but you also knew there was no way he could prove that. Despite Cayson's past, your decision was to give him a second chance, which, in my opinion, is commendable. But I suspect that whoever gave Cory the list to give you hoped that if you saw the details of Cayson's past in black and white, you might rethink things. I also think that whoever created the list realized that if they approached you and tried to force you to look at Cayson in the same light as this individual seems to, you would have refused to do so."

"I guess that much is true. There are a lot of rumors going around right now that can never be proven or disproven. I'm sure they'll eventually find Houghton's killer. Until then, I plan to merely stay the course." He looked directly at Dawson. "Any idea who gave Cory the list to give to me?"

"I suspect it was Lucas Manfield, but I can't prove that. What I do know is that Manfield has been outspoken about his desire to hang Cayson in the town square for crimes he likely got away with in the past, and I was able to determine that Cory is currently working a job with Manfield. The men have been seen together on the job and after hours on multiple occasions."

"That does fit," I said. I looked at Leo. "How are you feeling about this? Cory seemed to have given you the list to create doubt about your decision to hire Cayson. Did it work?"

"No. Not really. I guess the situation has caused me to stop and seriously think about things, but it truly does seem that Cayson is as much a victim here as anyone."

I looked at Dawson. "It seems that Lucas Manfield has a reason to frame Cayson. Can you think of a reason for Manfield to want to kill Houghton?"

"Not off hand, but Manfield as the killer is an interesting theory. One that I may take the time to look into."

Dawson and I had chatted with Leo for a while longer and were getting ready to leave when Alex walked in.

"As long as I caught you while you're all still together, I have something interesting to share," Alex said as she removed her badge and gun and set them on a nearby table.

"What sort of interesting news?" Leo asked after he greeted his girlfriend. "Does it have to do with Houghton's murder?"

"Not directly, but I can see how it might be related. After chatting with Beck yesterday, I asked for a copy of the police report filed by the state police at the time of Caleb's accident. It was on my desk when I went in after finishing up at the old seaport building. A cursory glance didn't reveal anything important. As we already knew, the determination of the cause of the accident was that the vehicle had drifted off the road and went over the side of the embankment, causing it to plunge to the bottom of the drop-off, where it exploded, killing the driver. It was outlined in the report that the car exploded on impact and that it burned hot, completely destroying the human remains as well as any other evidence that may have been left behind. The car fire started a brush fire, which was eventually spotted by a motorist on the highway and was called in. After the fire was extinguished, the car was identified due to the license plate found on the side of the hillside, which the investigator determined likely fell off as the car rolled down the embankment. Basically, the case was closed, and Nell was notified of her brother's death after a cursory investigation."

So far, we knew all of this, so I wasn't sure where Alex was going with her story, but we all just listened.

She continued. "There was one comment made by the fireman who filled out the report after arriving to battle the brush fire. His comment was that, based on the amount of destruction sustained by the vehicle, the fire must have burned hotter than it normally would have had gasoline been the only fuel to feed the fire. He tested the dirt in the area and found traces of nitroglycerine."

"Nitroglycerine, as in the thing that makes dynamite go boom?" Leo asked.

Alex smiled and nodded. "Exactly. In all honesty, if I hadn't just been at the scene of a dynamite stash I might not have given that small fact a second thought. But now? I have to admit that I'm wondering if the fact that nitroglycerin was at the scene of the accident isn't important."

"Do you think Caleb had dynamite in his car when the accident occurred?" Dawson asked.

"As I said, I didn't until we found the dynamite in the old seaport building today, but then it occurred to me that someone had to transport the explosives to get them there. Once the bomb squad showed up, they determined the explosives had been there for months."

"Based on what Dawson has uncovered so far, Caleb did need money," I said. "It sounds as if his job at the town offices may have put him in a position to meet and possibly even get to know the individuals behind the new development. Maybe they offered him cash to move the explosives into place."

"That was months ago. If Caleb moved the dynamite into the old seaport building, why hasn't anyone ignited it?" Leo asked.

Alex answered. "Caleb's accident might have brought too much attention to the entire idea of an explosion. If the old seaport building had been blown up right after the accident, someone might have noticed the link between the exploding car and fire at Juniper Ridge and an explosion at the old seaport building sooner."

"So they decided to wait," I said.

"That would be my guess," Alex responded.

"I assume that Colt knows about this," Dawson stated.

"He does," Alex confirmed. "He's working on getting more information on the dynamite. Where it came from and how long it's been stacked in the old seaport building." Alex looked at Dawson. "I'm pretty sure he'll call you to hack into whatever files you need to make sense of this whole thing."

"And where does Houghton fit into this?" I asked. "Was he in on the plan to blow up the old seaport building, or was he a pawn used to carry out a specific role?"

"I'm honestly not sure," Alex admitted. "The man seemed to have been working with the developer, but he also ended up dead."

"It did sound as if he'd been working with the developer, and, in fact, I seem to remember that he'd had a meeting set up with the developer on the day his body was found, but what if he'd started off being a supporter but then changed his mind. Might the developer have decided to eliminate him as a means of tying up loose ends?" I asked.

Alex frowned. "I agree that Houghton's death appears to be linked to the man who is trying to develop the old seaport, but I wouldn't discount other explanations at this point."

"What I don't get is Caleb's involvement, assuming we determine he was even involved," I said. "Why would this nice kid from Nebraska get wrapped up in blowing up a building?"

"Cold hard cash," Dawson suggested. "As previously discussed, Caleb was wrapped up in the online betting game, CHOMP." He looked at Alex. "I opened an account so that I'd have access to poke around, and I found that I can view the betting and winning activity of the other players. I can't actually log into their accounts, but I can see when they buy in, how many games they have chosen to participate in that week, and whether or not they are a winner in any of the games."

"So, do you have access to Caleb's account?" Alex asked.

"Not directly, but I hacked in and pulled up his historical games. It looks as if Caleb was betting heavily before his death. He was also regularly winning, but he wasn't winning as much as he lost, and, to me, it seemed unlikely that he'd have been able to stay afloat for long."

"So, as you explained it to me, he'd bet a thousand dollars across several games, and he might win five hundred in one of the games, but he'd still feel like a winner since he won money in one of the games even though he was down overall," I said.

"Exactly. It's a common trap for those with gambling addictions."

"So Caleb had lost a bunch of cash by the time he died," Leo clarified.

"He had," Dawson confirmed. "I wondered how he managed to stay with it as long as he had, but then I found out that, like many betting establishments, it's possible to play on credit, at least for a while. Of course, the interest on that credit is insane, and if you don't pay it back, the penalty can be deadly."

"So, did one of the thugs from CHOMP kill Caleb?" I asked.

Dawson shook his head. "No, at least I don't think so. Ultimately, they wanted their money, and Caleb was uniquely positioned to get it."

"Because of his job with the town," I said. "He could embezzle funds using his techy know-how, or he was in a position to find dirt on his colleagues, which he could use to blackmail them. Really, with his access to all the emails and files, he could have approached fundraising in several dissimilar ways."

"If the person who planned to blow up the old seaport building wanted to stay in hiding while things were put into place, then I guess hiring someone expendable to move the explosives might make sense," Alex said.

"Expendable? Are you saying that Caleb's accident was really a murder orchestrated to look like an accident?" I asked.

She shrugged. "We still don't know if the guy is dead or alive, but given everything else we've figured out, if he is dead, murder seems totally possible."

Alex needed to make a few calls, so Dawson and I headed home to clean up and change clothes. Since it looked like we'd be about thirty minutes late meeting Beck and Lou, Dawson called Beck to give him a heads-up. When Beck heard about the dynamite, he suggested we meet somewhere where having a good meal and talking freely was possible. After tossing a few locations into the mix, we decided on a steak house with large, well-spaced tables. Another reason the steak house was preferred was because it was far enough off the beaten path that it usually wasn't crowded, even on a Sunday.

"The old seaport building has been a hot topic lately," Lou commented once we'd filled Beck and Lou in on the afternoon's events. "I don't have all the details, but we have a few locals who are into the area's history, and I've sat in on a few discussions revolving around that old building. As you may know, it was built in the eighteen hundreds. In its heyday, it served as a prominent port of call along the eastern seaboard. The seaport's popularity diminished over time, and the building was used for various purposes. I understand it's been deserted for decades."

"Alex made a similar comment," I said. "It appears that a developer has purchased the land with plans to build a resort, upscale condos, or similar development, but a group has filed paperwork to protect the building due to its historical significance. I guess the whole thing has been tied up in court."

"I suppose that might explain the explosives," Beck said. "Blow up the building and blow up the court case."

We all agreed that the idea had likely been to move things along by taking the preservation of the building out of the equation.

"I knew Caleb," Lou shared. "Not well, but casually. He was a reader and stopped by every few weeks to check out the new arrivals. Sometimes, we'd chat. He was usually in a hurry, so we wouldn't chat long. Our conversations were fairly superficial and unrelated to anything we've been discussing, but I found the young man quite pleasant. When he died in that accident, I remember feeling sad. I also remember wondering why he'd been on the county road so late at night. Of course, I didn't know any of this, so I had no reason to suspect foul play of any sort, but his location at the time of the accident does beg the question of why. Even if he was transporting dynamite from another location to the old seaport building, which might explain why he was out in the middle of the night, why would he be all the way out there? Really, where could his trip with the dynamite have originated from that would take him on that route?"

"It does seem unlikely that the guy would have been traveling that road by chance, which makes the intentionally faked death theory all that more viable," Beck said.

"If the guy is alive and we can track him down, we could ask him what went on that night," I said. "If he's dead, we may never know what really went on."

"Have you had any luck with the facial recognition software?" Beck asked Dawson.

"Not yet."

"Is the software the sort where you can target a location?" Lou asked.

"It is," Dawson said. "Do you have a destination in mind?"

"Key West, Florida. I remember that Caleb was a bit of an armchair traveler. He'd tell me about the travel shows he'd seen on TV and the internet travel sites he enjoyed. He had a wide variety of interests, but he truly loved the sea and commented on more than one occasion that when he was done here, he was heading south to check out Key West."

"That sounds like a good tip," Dawson said. "I'll narrow my search and see what I turn up."

Chapter 12

The Key West tip ended up being just the thing to help us move on to the next step in our mission to determine whether Caleb was dead or alive without a shadow of a doubt. Dawson still hadn't gotten a hit with his facial recognition software, but Beck felt the tip was solid enough that he decided to fly down and check it out personally. Lou decided to go with him, which left Dawson and me to decide whether to try to relax or dig around in Lucas Manfield's life just a bit. After a brief discussion, we decided to dig into Lucas and any other suspects we might come up with, hoping that we would put this entire mystery and its individual parts to rest once and for all.

"So here's what we know," I said to Dawson over coffee that morning. "Gavin Houghton was found dead on Friday of last week. He was last seen on

Thursday. Before being murdered, he was working with the man who hopes to develop the old seaport. Due to the age and historical significance of the property, some people believe that the building should be protected, and a group has filed to have the development stopped, resulting in an ongoing court case."

Dawson picked up the thread. "This is an important pinpoint in the investigation into Houghton's death since it appears that, while Houghton was initially helping the developer to get the permits he needed to develop the land, the process might have been taking too long for the developer's taste, and the man may have taken matters into his own hands."

"If our assumption is that the developer is the person who filled the old seaport building with dynamite to bring down the building, then I agree that's likely. If this turns out to be the case, then Houghton may have waffled at some point, which I suppose I can understand. Helping the developer to bypass the normal permit process is one thing, but blowing up a building is something else altogether."

Dawson agreed. "In this scenario, I suppose the developer, or more likely, someone who works for the developer, would be the killer. I'm not sure why someone with no current links to the town other than land ownership would even think to frame Cayson, but the rest works okay. Still, ultimately, I think we need to find a suspect who not only wanted Houghton dead but also wanted Cayson framed for it."

I took a sip of my coffee, taking a moment to think things over. "We know that Lucas Manfield has a huge problem with Cayson living and working in our town, so I can see him framing Cayson, but I'm not sure why he'd kill Houghton. It seemed that the two men were friends. Houghton seemed to hate Cayson as much as Manfield did, so killing Houghton doesn't really fit the overall scenario where Manfield is the bad guy."

Dawson leaned back in his chair. "It looks as if we have a man with a possible reason to want Houghton out of the way, who, at least on the surface, has no real reason to frame Cayson and a man who seems to have a reason to frame Cayson, who, on the surface, has no real reason to kill Houghton."

"I suppose Manfield might have simply taken advantage of the situation caused by Houghton's death," I said. "The man has been outspoken about his displeasure in sharing his living and working space with a man who may or may not have killed someone in his past. Even before Houghton died and his body was found wrapped in Cayson's rug, Manfield was responsible for the signs at Leo's job site as well as other signs around town. I also heard he's been hosting rallies to get other town members worked up enough to toss the guy."

"And he also seems to be behind the list of names Leo was given and the graffiti on Cayson's garage," Dawson pointed out.

"The fact that the guy wants Cayson gone is no secret, but to kill the town manager to accomplish that? It doesn't add up."

Dawson blew out a long breath. "Yeah, I agree, it really doesn't fit. And, the developer being the individual behind the idea to frame Cayson doesn't fit either. Unless…"

"Unless what?" I asked.

"Unless the developer hired someone to kill Houghton, who somehow happened to know Cayson."

"Like a former cellmate or someone else from his criminal past," I speculated.

Dawson nodded. "It might be an idea worth looking into. We've said from the beginning that if the developer is the person behind Houghton's death, he wouldn't get his own hands dirty. If he hired someone who just happened to know Cayson to get rid of Houghton, and if this individual knew about the conflict created when Cayson decided to stay in Holiday Bay after being released from prison, he may have decided to use that to both divert attention from the developer and to get back at someone who may have wronged him at some point."

I liked the theory, but how would we prove any of this?

"The killer has to have had access to Cayson's shed, which is where both the rug used to wrap the body and the bat likely used to beat the man to death were stored," I pointed out. "Cayson admitted that there was just a bunch of junk in the shed that his mother had saved, so it wasn't locked, but the killer would still have needed to know the rug and bat were there."

"I suppose it would be easy enough to find out where Cayson lived once the killer realized he was in town," Dawson suggested. "From there, he'd just need to wait for Cayson to go to work and then help himself to whatever he felt he could use."

I supposed that Dawson had a valid point, and the killer might have simply used the props that had happened to be in the shed to set up the frame. "While it is possible the motive for Houghton's murder was of a personal nature, to me, it seems that given his job title and his reputation for being on the take, the motive for his murder is more likely to be work-related," I said. "When I spoke to Charise, whose husband is an attorney who regularly golfs with the town's attorney, she said that Houghton was bad news. She flat out said that he operated outside the bounds of the law at times, especially if it meant financial gain, but also said that she'd never publicly admit that she'd overheard the conversations she had. At the time, she had identified River Overland as a suspect, whom we have since ruled out. There must, however, be others. I wonder if another discussion with her would do us any good."

"I guess a friendly, nonconfrontational conversation might not hurt. You could call Charise and pretend that there's an issue about something related to the event in May. Then, while you're on the phone, you could casually comment about the lead involving River not working out and ask if she had anyone else she would look at if she was the one conducting the investigation."

I smiled. "That should work."

Even though it was early, it wasn't so early that Charise would still be in bed, so I went ahead and called her. If she wasn't into sharing, I supposed she'd say so. As I hoped she would, she answered right away. I made up something about having problems getting some ingredients for the dessert she requested and asked if she had a backup just in case. She offered a couple of suggestions, and then I brought up the Gavin Houghton murder case.

"I heard about the explosives," she said. "I can't believe that wacko was planning to blow up that building."

"While we don't know that Houghton planned to blow up the building, I guess that's possible, but there are other ways of looking at things. One of the theories being floated around is that in the beginning, Houghton had been helping Jethro Paul, but the men had a falling out, and Houghton changed course. In this scenario, Paul was the person who planned to blow up the building."

"Doubtful, but I guess possible. I guarantee you that Houghton could be bought, and as long as the money kept flowing, his commitment was solid. Having said that, Houghton never struck me as the sort of person to have an ounce of loyalty to anyone. If you were the highest bidder for his services, he would definitely be on your side."

"So if someone who was against the development of the land where the old seaport building sits offered Houghton more money to jump over to their side than the developer was offering him to support the development, he likely would have jumped."

"He most certainly would have jumped. Or he would have used his leverage to get more cash out of Paul. I suppose that I can see that going either way."

It did sound like the developer could be the killer, but again, we needed to figure out how the whole Cayson thing figured in.

"Would you be willing to give me your thoughts if I told you something confidential?" I asked.

"I suppose. But again, I need to be careful about what I publicly admit to knowing or not knowing. My husband's career and my quality of life depend on a certain amount of discretion."

"I understand. I'm really just asking for you to take a guess at something."

"Okay. What's on your mind?"

"Those of us investigating the murder in an attempt to help Cayson have suspected that the developer, or someone working for the developer, killed Houghton, but we haven't been able to figure out a link between the developer and Cayson. Any ideas?"

She hesitated. I suspected she knew something but was trying to decide what to say or perhaps what not to say.

"The fact that you and I had this hypothetical discussion can stay between you and me. I'm not asking you to share anything told to you in confidence, but simply asking you to guess what sort of relationship might exist between Cayson and

Jethro Paul or someone working for Jethro Paul," I persuaded.

"Kevin Devine. That's all I can say."

With that, she hung up.

Kevin Devine? The name didn't sound familiar, but I supposed that Dawson could do a search. As it turned out, to this point, Kevin Devine was definitely the best lead we'd had.

Chapter 13

Dawson was able to determine that Kevin Devine was a contract killer who was currently incarcerated for a drive-by shooting that killed a Maryland state senator's son. The murder occurred almost ten years ago, and it looked as if Kevin was going to slip under the radar and get away with it, as he had done dozens of times in the past. But then Kevin was arrested for acting as the getaway guy in an armed robbery seven months ago. While he was in prison for his role in the armed robbery, which would likely only have resulted in about five years served with good behavior, Devine made a mistake and told one of his prison mates about killing the senator's son. The prison mate then used this information to work out a deal, and Devine was currently sentenced to life in prison.

"Maryland," Beck said when I shared this information with him over the phone. "Cayson was sent to prison for the death of a clerk during a robbery in Baltimore, which is also in Maryland. Kevin Devine must have shared space with him."

"He did. And while we haven't proven anything yet, it seems that Cayson might have been the one to give him up. If that's the case, I'm surprised that Cayson isn't dead, but maybe Devine knew that life in prison was even worse than death, so he cooperated in a plan to get him put back behind bars."

"That all fits, but since Devine is in prison, he couldn't have killed Houghton or framed Cayson," Beck pointed out.

"Dawson thinks that it was a buddy of Devine's who likely did the deed. Devine was a contract killer for a couple decades. I'm sure he formed many alliances along the way. He may even know Jethro Paul, and when Paul needed someone to clean up the mess he made with Houghton, perhaps he asked Devine to recommend someone. If Devine recommended someone he was tight with, framing Cayson for the murder might actually have been part of the package."

"I guess it might have played out that way. It seems that the first step is to conclusively link Cayson and Devine," Beck suggested.

"Alex went to talk to Cayson. If he admits he was released from prison early for snitching on Devine, we'll have something to work with."

"Being released from prison early seems like a reasonable deal to have made, but an expulsion of his record relating to the murder in Baltimore? It just seems that there must be more going on."

"Maybe, but if Cayson possessed information that could aid in solving an old cold case involving a senator's son, I'm betting he had a lot of bargaining power."

"I guess he did at that," Beck admitted.

"So, how are things there? Have you tracked down Caleb?"

"Not yet, but we're working on it. We had a couple people say they might have seen someone who somewhat looked like him, but we haven't come up with any solid leads. Lou and I will be here until Wednesday morning. If he's here, we'll find him, and if he's not, we will have had a nice trip in a gorgeous location."

"I guess it's a win-win sort of situation. Stay in touch."

"I will. And Shelby."

"Yeah."

"If you all plan to take on a contract killer, be careful."

"I personally plan to let the police handle it, but yeah, we'll be careful."

With that, I hung up.

Dawson was out on the patio chatting with Leo while we waited for Alex to return from her chat with Cayson. I decided to join the men.

"Has Beck had any luck?" Dawson asked.

"Not yet, but he's working on it. He was concerned that we're poking around in a case that might involve a contract killer and wants us to be careful."

"Alex and I discussed the idea of calling in the FBI if Cayson can confirm enough of our theory to make it viable," Leo informed me. "At this point, all we have is a good idea. We'll need more."

"Have you spoken to Colt about it?" I wondered.

"We have, and he agrees that if it looks like Houghton was killed by one of Devine's cronies, then bringing in the big guns would be the best idea."

"That land where the old seaport building sits must be really valuable to go to so much trouble," I told the men. "If Jethro Paul did hire a paid killer to take out Houghton rather than just using one of his own thugs to handle the deed, he must have had a reason for going to such lengths."

"It does sort of seem like overkill," Leo admitted. "And most contract killers just shoot their intended victim and move on. I can understand why the guy might have done things the way he has if framing Cayson was the intention, but it still feels off to me."

"Maybe we're just off chasing windmills with this one," Dawson suggested. "At this point, I guess all we can do is follow each lead as we get it and then move on to the next lead if the previous one doesn't pan out."

I looked at Leo. "Has Alex mentioned whether or not the local police have any official suspects we haven't considered? I know our little group has been working on it with limited success, but I'm sure that Colt and Alex have been working on Houghton's death in an official capacity."

"Alex hasn't mentioned anyone by name, but I know that interviews have been conducted and leads have been established and followed up on. Alex can't always talk about what she's doing in an official capacity, but I can tell that she's frustrated. I'm sure Colt and Brax are as well. When I told her about Kevin Devine, she was very excited by the lead. Which, to me, indicates that, like our little group, the police haven't gotten anywhere either."

The more I thought about Kevin Devine, the more of a long shot I felt it might be, but it was still something, and at this point, we really didn't have anything better. I offered Leo and Dawson some iced tea, and I had just entered the kitchen to get it when I heard a car in the drive. I hoped it was Alex with good news.

"Cayson wouldn't share a thing about the terms of his release, but he did say that his release didn't involve Devine in any way and that there was no way Kevin Devine was involved in Houghton's murder," Alex shared once she'd settled onto the patio, and I'd offered her a beverage. "According to Cayson, Houghton is small-town potatoes while Devine is contract killer royalty even though he was currently residing in a maximum-security prison. He felt certain that killing Houghton, no matter how much cash was involved, was beneath him."

"And framing him?" I asked. "Wasn't Cayson concerned that the man might want to enact some sort of revenge?"

Alex answered. "Like I said, Cayson indicated that his release didn't involve Devine, so Devine would have no reason to want to frame him. He thinks we're barking up the wrong tree even though our logic wasn't half bad."

"It looks as if we're back to square one," Leo said.

"Not necessarily," Alex said. "Cayson did admit that he'd been thinking about the fact that Houghton's murder seemed to have been intended to accomplish two things. One, of course, was to get rid of Houghton, but the other was to frame him. He's been thinking of that and endeavoring to determine who hated him enough that they would go to so much effort. As we've already discussed, if someone really wanted him gone, killing him would be much easier than framing him, so the person we were looking for needed a fairly specific reason for doing what they'd been doing."

"Did he come up with anyone?" I asked.

"Actually, he came up with several names, but he'd already poked around and decided he was off course. There was one name that seemed to have staying power, however. Gifford Bowden."

"Gifford Bowden? Charise Bowden's husband?" I asked.

She nodded. "According to Cayson, Bowden was a juvenile prosecutor who had his eye on the district attorney's job when Cayson was living in Holiday Bay as a child and teen. On numerous occasions, Bowden tried to get Cayson jail time for the petty crimes he was constantly being arrested for, but Cayson's mom was friends with the judge on the bench at the time, so Bowden never did manage to get him tossed in the slammer. Cayson admitted this frustrated Bowden to no end. He also admitted that he hadn't done anything to help himself and had, in fact, been quite unpleasant and a considerable mess when he was young. Cayson even went so far as to admit that Bowden might not have been wrong to want him to suffer for his actions. Of course, he didn't see things that way as a teen. He, in fact, saw Bowden's witch hunt as a personal vendetta, so he decided to make it personal in return and began bullying Bowden's son, who was his age."

"Bowden's son is Cayson's age? I thought Charise's children were younger," I said.

"They are. Charise is Bowden's second wife. The son Cayson tormented as a teen was a child from Bowden's first marriage. Cayson said that Bowden's son, Arnie, had left Holiday Bay immediately after graduating high school."

"Okay," Dawson said. "It does seem that Gifford Bowden might have reason to want Cayson locked up. He probably considers it unfair that Cayson was tried and convicted of a crime he only had to serve a few years for. But would he kill Houghton?"

Alex answered. "Not personally, but Gifford is representing Jethro Paul in the lawsuit brought against Paul's company over the planned demolition of the old seaport building. Cayson suggested that Bowden might have happened to catch wind of a plan by the developer to off the town manager, who he suspected had turned the tables on them, and may have suggested they frame Cayson for the murder as long as they were at it."

"That's actually a theory that works," Dawson said.

"I thought so," Alex agreed. "I called Colt. He's going to meet me at the office so we can discuss the situation. Colt mentioned bringing Gifford in for questioning, although I doubt the man will admit to anything."

Everyone said that sounded like the best plan at this point. I stood up to walk Alex out when a hawk landed on a tree branch only inches from where I was standing. *Avoid distraction and focus on your intuition*, I thought to myself. I still wasn't sure exactly what that meant, but I decided to go with an idea that had popped into my head. "Before you meet with Colt, we should probably discuss the idea that Charise might have been feeding me red herrings to chase all along. Her tips seemed like good information at the time, but none of them have actually gone anywhere."

"So you think she's in on things?" Alex asked.

"I think she may know more than she's let on." I paused and tried to focus my thoughts. "I haven't figured this all out, but my intuition is adamantly telling me that it might benefit us to have a conversation with Charise. Give her a chance to tell us what she knows before Colt speaks to her husband."

Alex looked uncertain, but eventually, she agreed to call Colt and run the idea past him. Colt admitted that Charise had been helpful in a very unhelpful sort of way and that perhaps a conversation with Charise might not be a bad idea. It was decided that Alex and I would go and chat with Charise while Colt and Brax had an equally frank conversation with Gifford.

After a bit of discussion, it was decided that I would call Charise and use a potential problem with the booster club luncheon to get Charise out of her house and to the Bistro, where we felt she might be more receptive to the conversation Alex and I planned to have with her. Once Charise showed up, Alex and I asked her to sit in the dining room, which was empty since the Bistro was closed on Mondays.

"What's this all about?" Charise demanded. She looked at me. "I thought you wanted to discuss a problem with the luncheon."

"I actually just used that to get you down here," I admitted. I glanced at Alex. She nodded. "The police are questioning Gifford as we speak. Apparently, they found evidence that the two of you worked together to kill Houghton and frame Cayson."

"What?" The woman's eyes frantically darted around as if looking for an escape route. "I don't know what you think you know, but I can tell you in no uncertain terms that you're wrong."

"The reason I'm here," Alex said, "is to provide you with an opportunity to tell your side of the story before your husband throws you under the bus."

Her eyes flashed in anger. "Gifford wouldn't do that."

"Even if he was offered leniency in exchange for his testimony?" Alex asked.

I watched as fear replaced the anger in Charise's eyes.

"You can trust Alex to do what's right by you, but you need to tell us what you know," I said with as much encouragement in my tone as I could muster. "This is your only chance to tell your side of the story. If I were you, I'd take advantage of the opportunity before it's gone."

I could tell that she was considering the idea. Her eyes darted around the room before eventually settling on me. "I didn't kill anyone."

"I believe you," Alex said. "Why don't you tell me what did happen."

Charise began to cry. "The whole thing is such a big mess. I guess I did intentionally mislead you to keep you busy chasing down false leads, but I didn't actually lie. I said that Houghton was the sort who could be bought, and he was. I said that River had a problem with Houghton, and he did."

"So you shared selective truths, attempting to keep us busy," I said.

She nodded.

"Okay, go on. Since you fed me red herrings, what's really going on?"

She took in a deep breath and then answered. "I don't have all the details, but I do know that Jethro Paul paid Houghton to help him push through the paperwork required to have the old seaport building torn down after he bought the land on either side of the acreage where it sits. Houghton agreed to work with Paul to get things fast-tracked, but then the conservationist and historical society people got involved, and a lawsuit was filed. My husband was hired to represent Paul, which is how he got involved in the first place."

She stopped talking, so I encouraged her to continue.

"In the beginning, it seemed as if Houghton was all in, but then something happened to cause him to waver. Paul could tell that Houghton was having second thoughts, so he had his thug kill him. Framing Cayson was Gifford's idea." She looked directly at me. "Don't judge Gifford for that. He has a history with the man who, if Gifford is to be believed, is a truly horrible person."

"So, was the part about Cayson helping you when your car slid off the road and became stuck in a snowbank a lie?" I asked.

"That much was true, and when I mentioned to Gifford what a nice man he was, my husband told me the rest. Apparently, as a teen, Cayson not only ignored the law, causing him all sorts of headaches, but he tortured his son. The things my husband shared with me were horrible and convinced me that the man would never learn his lesson until he was made to pay for what he'd done."

I was going to respond, but Alex, who seemed more on track than I was, took control of the situation. "You said that Houghton was on board with helping Jethro Paul, but something happened. What exactly happened?"

She hesitated.

"We can finish this here, or we can finish this down at the station," Alex warned.

The woman swallowed hard. "Caleb Farmer happened."

"Go on," Alex persuaded.

She hesitated again, but Alex waited her out this time, and eventually, she began to speak. "Paul was getting tired of waiting for the demolition project to be approved, so he came up with the idea of blowing the place up, thereby taking any court rulings that may damn him up out of the equation. Since the guy was smart enough not to personally be involved in the old seaport building's demolition, he decided to hire one person to deliver a van with the dynamite to the building and hire someone else to ignite the explosives. Houghton knew that Caleb was in real trouble with some exceedingly bad people due to a gambling debt he'd racked up, so he decided to approach him about picking up the explosives and delivering them to the building. Caleb only needed to deliver the dynamite from the warehouse, where he picked it up, to the old seaport building and wasn't tasked with detonating the explosives. I imagine the fact that Houghton offered him enough to pay off his debt propelled him to agree to take the job."

Since Alex indicated there hadn't been a van on the property, I assumed that Caleb or someone else had unloaded it.

"Go on," Alex said.

I handed the woman a tissue since the tears were freely flowing down her cheeks by this point. She thanked me and then continued.

"When Caleb got to the old seaport building and saw people living there, I guess he had second thoughts. He left the van where he was told to leave it, but rather than just cashing in his payday and paying off his debt, he sought out Houghton to tell him about it. Keep in mind that Houghton was his boss, and the two men were friends of sorts. Caleb told Houghton about the people living in the old seaport building. It seemed like Caleb assumed that no one knew of their presence and that the entire operation would be halted once Houghton was informed that there were inhabitants in the building."

"But that wasn't what happened," Alex said.

She shook her head. "No, that wasn't what happened. Paul felt that moving the homeless population to another location would draw attention to the property. He didn't want anyone watching the place before the deed was done, so, in the end, he decided to sacrifice Caleb."

"So Paul had him killed," I confirmed.

She nodded. "At this point, I want it to be perfectly clear that Jethro Paul's actions were entirely his own. Houghton didn't know about the plan to eliminate Caleb ahead of time, nor did my husband. Paul had one of his thugs do the deed, and no one I know of outside his inner circle knew about it until after it was done."

"What exactly was done?" I asked. "Caleb's accident appeared to have been just that."

Charise answered. "Paul had a couple of his thugs detain Caleb, and then they used his car to drive him to Juniper Ridge. The vehicle, which had been loaded with dynamite, was then pushed over the ledge. The impact with the rocks at the bottom of the drop-off took care of the rest."

"So the remains found in the car were Caleb's remains," I said, feeling an overwhelming sense of loss and sadness.

"They were. I know you've been going around looking for an alternative explanation. I, however, personally overheard my husband talking to Houghton about it before Houghton died, so I know for a fact that Caleb was the one to die."

I supposed I'd need to let Beck know that his errand would never turn anything up.

Once again, Alex brought the conversation back to the matter at hand. "So Jethro Paul had Caleb killed, which caused Houghton to have second thoughts about siding with him on the seaport project. Then what?"

Charise paused and then answered. "I'm not exactly sure, but I know that Houghton came and spoke to my husband, who we've already established was representing Paul in the lawsuit brought forth by those wanting to save that old building. Rather than siding with Houghton, as Houghton seemed to hope he would do, I'm afraid my husband only warned Houghton about the ramifications of telling anyone what he knew. It appeared that Houghton continued to toe the line for a while, but, in the end, he was killed as well. I don't have all the details relating to Houghton's death. I only know that while my husband didn't kill Houghton, it was my husband's idea to frame Cayson."

"Why did you go along with things?" I asked. "Why try to send me on wild goose chases?"

"I don't know. My husband asked me to keep you and your little group busy while he could figure things out. I didn't really lie, and I didn't believe I was causing harm to anyone, although now I realize that may not be entirely accurate." She wiped the tears from her face. "You have to understand that even though I wasn't directly involved in any of this, I did have a stake in it. Everything I have is due to my husband and his career, my entire life, my home, my community projects, and my elevated standard of living. He warned me that turning him in and telling what I knew would come at a great personal cost." She looked around the room. "I suspect that personal cost is inevitable at this point."

Alex decided it was time to call Colt and bring him up to speed. He suggested that she bring Charise to the station so they could get a formal statement. Colt sent Brax to bring Gifford in, and he called the county office so they could send a representative to help negotiate a deal for Charise. Jethro Paul lived in New York, so the FBI was also called in. Since I'd driven my car to the Bistro, I headed home once Alex left with Charise.

Chapter 14

A Week Later

The week that followed my conversation with Charise was intense. Dawson had volunteered to call Beck to fill him in on the news that we had an even better reason to believe that Caleb was actually dead than we'd had before. He admitted that he'd reached the same conclusion and that he and Lou hoped they could spend a few more days in Key West before coming home as long as Dawson and I were okay with dog-sitting Meatball for a few extra days. Of course, Dawson and I were always happy to dog-sit Meatball, who really was the sweetest thing, and it sounded as if Beck and Lou were having a wonderful time. I found myself wishing that Dawson and I had time to take a trip to somewhere exotic. Maybe we could once I found and hired a dining room manager.

In terms of Gavin Houghton's murder, Gifford Bowden had been arrested and was being held by the FBI while they researched the situation further, and Charise had been questioned by Colt and then released. I didn't have all the details on the Jethro Paul case, but Alex assured me that the FBI was putting together the proof they'd need to send Jethro Paul away for a very long time.

Things on the home front had definitely changed. Amy was completely moved out, leaving Dawson and me alone in our home. Sage wouldn't be back for at least a few months, and Sierra indicated that she likely wouldn't visit until mid-summer. While it felt odd for Dawson, Goliath, Hennessy, Marley, and me to have the house to ourselves, I was learning to appreciate the quiet and wondered if a reality existed where I'd actually want to return to chaos. Maybe if Dawson and I ever decided to have children, which I realized was a musing for another day.

"Did you hear about Cayson?" Alex asked me after she stopped at my house on her way to work when she noticed me sitting on the patio.

"No. What's going on with Cayson?"

"He's leaving town."

Okay, that surprised me. "Leaving? Why? He was totally cleared of everything."

"I didn't speak with him, but he spoke to Leo. I guess Cayson shared with Leo that this situation he'd found himself in this past few weeks had made him realize that it had been a mistake to come back to Holiday Bay in the first place. Cayson admitted to Leo that he hadn't been a good person when he lived here as a teen, and even though he'd changed, it was apparent that some people here remembered the bully he'd been. He shared that if he truly wanted to start over, he needed to start somewhere fresh. Somewhere where he didn't have a past to outrun."

I supposed I could understand that.

"So, what's going to happen with your rescue project?"

Alex smiled. "The good news is that Leo spoke to Nick, who eventually agreed to see it through. Nick is a loner who likes to work on his own renovation projects at his own pace rather than as part of a team, but however you dice it, he's also a heck of a contractor. Leo appealed to his altruistic side, and Nick eventually admitted that he hadn't started his most recent project yet and could probably do our project first. Since Cayson had a crew in place, Nick won't need to worry about hiring anyone, and Lonnie Parker agreed to help Nick as much as his schedule would allow. Leo is confident we're still on track to open in the fall as planned."

"That's wonderful. I feel bad for Cayson, but maybe starting over in a location where no one knows about his past will give him the fresh start he's hoping for."

"I hope so. Cayson really is a good guy."

"Can I get you some coffee?"

"No, but thanks. I'm heading to work. The reason I stopped in the first place was to ask about Nell. I never did speak with Beck after he returned from Key West and was curious how she took the news that her brother actually was dead."

I answered. "Beck said she seemed to take it okay. She admitted that her idea that her brother was alive was a bit of a long shot all along, but it was a long shot she needed to chase. Now that she has confirmation that he actually did die in the crash, I think she will be able to move on with her life."

"In a way, I guess Caleb was the one who saved the old seaport building and the people who were living there. Another dynamite delivery person might have dropped off the explosives and left, and the building and those inside would be nothing more than a memory at this point."

I supposed Alex had a point. While Caleb's reason for taking the job in the first place was less than honorable, he was a hero in the end.

Alex and I chatted for a few more minutes, and then she left. I thought about going inside, but it was such a pleasant morning, and the Bistro was closed today, so taking a moment with my thoughts wasn't a bad idea.

I watched as a pair of red-tailed hawks circled overhead. I'd been reading about hawks since my recent encounters had caused me to pause and take note, and I remembered reading that red-tailed hawks mated for life. In the past, I'd seen the pair around and hoped they planned to set up housekeeping here on my property. I thought about the increase in hawk activity and how it seemed to correspond with Dawson becoming such a significant part of my life. Would we, like the hawks, end up being lifetime partners? I supposed only time would tell.

"Is something on your mind?" Dawson asked after coming out of the house and sitting next to me.

"I was just watching the hawks."

He looked up. "I've noticed that the pair has been hanging around lately. I suspect they may have a nest in the area."

"I hope so. I enjoy having the hawks as neighbors."

"They do have a sort of soothing energy. Did you know that they mate for life?"

I smiled. "I heard that."

Dawson reached over and took my hand in his. "I wonder if the arrival of the hawks is a message of sorts."

I turned and looked at him. "Message?" I'd discussed the spirit animal idea with Nikki and Beck but not with Dawson; of course, I supposed either Nikki or Beck might have said something to him.

"I guess it just occurred to me that having the hawk couple set up residence here on the property at the same time that you and I are setting up our own residence might indicate that we're on target. It's nice to think that we're walking down the right path and that the universe supports us." He smiled. "I guess that sounds sort of fanciful."

I leaned over and gently kissed Dawson on the cheek. "Not at all. In fact, the idea of our hawk couple showing up to build a life together alongside the life we plan to build together sounds just about perfect."

USA Today best-selling author Kathi Daley lives in beautiful Lake Tahoe with her husband, Ken. When she isn't writing, she likes spending time hiking the miles of desolate trails surrounding her home. Find out more about her books at **www.kathidaley.com**

Made in United States
North Haven, CT
17 February 2025

66005053R00104